Praise for *The Maid's Tale*

"The author . . . has taken the Irish cliché of the
priest's housekeeper and made it literature."
– *Irish Independent*

"*The Maid's Tale* is splendid and awesome."
– Benedict Kiely

"This is more than a promising debut: it is a triumphant one."
– *Daily Telegraph*

"Reading it was an experience I shall not easily forget."
– David Marcus

"Ferguson negotiates the difficult narrative path she
has chosen with skill, freshness and humour."
– Arminta Wallace, *The Irish Times*

"This powerful debut novel . . . unfolds the story of Northern
Ireland in the past thirty five years."
– *Daily Mail*

Winner of
The Irish Times Irish Literature Prize for Fiction 1995

Shortlisted for the
Whitbread First Novel Award

Kathleen Ferguson was born in Tamnaherin, County Derry. She was educated at the University of Ulster, where she later taught English literature. She now writes full-time.

The Maid's Tale won *The Irish Times Irish Literature Prize for Fiction* 1995 and was shortlisted for the *Whitbread First Novel Award.*

The Maid's Tale

KATHLEEN FERGUSON

POOLBEG

First published 1994
by Torc
123 Baldoyle Industrial Estate
Dublin 13, Ireland
This edition published by
Poolbeg Press Ltd 1995
Reprinted September 1995
Reprinted October 1995

© Kathleen Ferguson 1994

The moral right of the author has been asserted.

The Publishers gratefully acknowledge the support of
The Northern Ireland Arts Council.

A catalogue record for this book is available from the British Library.

ISBN 1 85371 262 0

Cover painting: *Ancient Rubbish, Kilmurry* by Mildred Anne Butler,
courtesy of The National Gallery of Ireland
Cover design by Poolbeg Group Services Ltd
Printed by The Guernsey Press Ltd,
Vale, Guernsey, Channel Islands.

For my mother

Cavan County Library
Withdrawn Stock

CHAPTER ONE

The Catholic Church was father, mother and family to me for over fifty years. You can imagine what I felt, then, when the Bishop dropped me like that—like yesterday's newspaper he'd throw at his backside whenever he'd done with it. After I'd given Father Mann what many a wife never give her husband. For thirty-three years I washed Father's socks and made his bed. For thirty-three years I sweated over a hot stove for him, and ate his leftovers, and that on my own, in the kitchen, while he ate off a table-cloth in the dining room. But I've only myself to blame. I stayed long after I should've gone.

I was brought up in Bethel House, an orphanage run by the Sisters of Charity in Derry, though I wasn't an orphan strictly speaking. My ma was dead right enough. The story is my da give her a hiding she never got over. But he was still living, in Gransha mental hospital, where they'd shut him away for life. I had a sister Dympna, five years older than me, and a brother Michael, a couple of years older than that.

Bethel House was divided into two halves, one for the girls and the other for the boys. Dympna and me lived in one half, near hand the convent, and Michael lived in the other beside the Bishop's house. There wasn't much coming and going between the two. The nuns didn't allow it for fear of what might happen. So the three of us didn't grow up as a family. Come to that, I hardly knew much difference between Dympna

1

and the other girls I lived with. Family, in the sense most people understand the word, meant nothing to me. I didn't miss it. As far as I was concerned the words Mother and Sister was meant for nuns, not for blood relations. What the nuns told me—that the Church was my mother and God was my father—I swallowed.

I never thought of Bethel House as an orphanage at the time I was living there. The word seemed too old-fashioned, like some place in the novels the teacher used to make us read at school. It brought to mind pictures of skinny youngsters shivering with fear and hunger, which was a far cry from the way things really was. I never wanted in Bethel House. At least, I never went cold nor hungry. But I'll tell you this much, my mind took fifty years to get free. Many as grew up with me wasn't near as lucky. Like the bulk brought up in institutions in my time, 'specially institutions run by the Catholic Church, they never managed to escape; not really. We were made to feel we didn't belong in the outside world from the start. Nothing was said to us, but it was got through our heads some way or another we weren't fit to be wives and mothers. As far back as I can mind, I had the notion marriage was a bad thing. Marriage was for other women, outside the House, and men. It's hard to believe now, but this was happening in the Fifties, when the way you looked was everything.

The Sisters ran the primary school in Bishop Street, and Thornhead School—for girls—where I went after that. They were aye scrounging money off relatives to build extensions. I felt a wild pity for the relatives for they couldn't rightly refuse when asked bare-faced like that. The two schools took in youngsters from outside the House as well as us from inside, but it was at Thornhead I got my first real taste of the outside world.

2

I was singled out from the beginning, and pestered and bullied. The ringleader among the bullies was Magdalene Cooke, a big, beefy girl with a plain face and mousy hair. It occurred to me at the time her parents must've been terrible disappointed with Magdalene, for she was the only girl they had and I guessed by her name they had high hopes for her. Her best friend was Mary Healy. Now, Mary Healy would've slit her own wrists if Magdalene Cooke had asked her to. She was that scared Magdalene would take up with somebody else instead of her. The reason for this was her da had run off to Liverpool with another woman, you see, and Mary stuck like glue to people for fear they'd go away and leave her too. She took it out of Magdalene sometimes, I could see that—the way she hung round her neck. In looks, Mary was awful peaky. She had this thin skin the colour of rice-paper, and freckles just like a wee fella, and pooky hair that aye stood on end even when it rained. Then there was Bernie Sheedy, the pretty one among them. The low, sneakin' sort she was, Bernie Sheedy only ever joined in when the others had the better of me. The second Bernadette was Bernadette Ratty. (There was four in the class on account of a diocesan pilgrimage to Lourdes the year we were all born.) Bernadette Ratty had sticking-out teeth and eyes that nearly met in the middle of her face. Like the others, this one had it in her to be vicious, but she didn't have the gumption to lay into me on her own. As much as she could do was call me names. She was a hanger-on. And there was others too. But these four give me the hardest time.

The chapel, which was up the lane from the school, was a good hiding place for some of the nuns was aye praying there. During lunch-time I'd go off there on my own to have my lunch. I got the name of being holy that way, I think. I mind one day in particular. I was sixteen at the time, and in the fifth year. It was a sharp December day. Thinking back on it now, I can almost feel the cold of the water-font against my fingertips. I tip-toed into the chapel, a habit I learned before I can remember. (I still hush my step in a chapel for fear of the silence.) As usual, I knelt down in the back seat and threw my school-bag on the seat in front of me. Some new writing had been added to that already on the bag. Whoever had done it had dug into the leather with black biro. "Have you been, Shamey? Have you been?" That's what they'd written. Shamey was my nick-name, you see. Magdalene Cooke had got it off a simpleton in a play that was on radio some time before. "Have you been?" meant have you been to the toilet. That was a line from the play.

For the life of me, I couldn't understand why they called me Shamey, a man's name of all names. Why not Mad Martha or Baby Jane if they wanted to make out I was demented? But I didn't give anything much thought in them days. Bad things just happened to me and I lay down and took them like the stoodgy I was. Thirty-three years had to go by before I could bring my mind to bear on them. Since then I put this much the-gether. I was a loner. I hadn't any friends at the time I'm talking about, not that that bothered me any, but it bothered Magdalene and her friends. The quare kind they were, they thought a person was rare that was content enough to be alone. Being on my own made me an easy target into the bargain, a target for anyone needing a guilt-offering. And Thornhead, take my word for it, was full of people needing guilt-offerings. Girls growing up in a convent school, in a Catholic town, with not a soul they could trust to talk to. They were scared stiff, many of them, and didn't like what was happening to them and they turned their fears and frustrations on me. I'd grown up earlier than most of them, you see, by which I mean I'd had my periods while I was still in primary school. I was wearing a 34C bra by the time I'm talking about and this made them terrible jealous. It made them mad, as well, that I didn't open my mouth about sex or even seem to think about it. Either that or they took me for a prig and wanted to rub my nose in it. The week before, three of them had shoved me down on the ground and pushed handfuls of grass inside my shirt. They followed me to the toilet for months at one time. Taking up the cubicles on either side of me, they'd climb on the toilet bowl and peer over the partition walls. They never give me no peace. As you can imagine, this helped my shyness none. And I was terrible shy. Knowing no better, Magdalene and the rest took this shyness for backwardness and called me after a simpleton. I figure they called me after a man because I was different from them. I wasn't the only woman in the school with a man's name, of course. Some of the sisters had men's names too—like Sister Aloysius and Sister Christopher. (Magdalene Cooke maintained they weren't proper women.) I think I was bearing the brunt for them. And I was bearing the brunt for men as well. By punishing Shamey, Magdalene and the rest was getting their own back on all the boys and men that ever give them a hard time. They had a right to be angry too, for the Catholic Church give women a hard time. I see that much now. Saint Augustine says a woman "casts down the mind of man." As for Saint Paul—well I won't start on him! Being born a woman wasn't a thing to be proud or pleased about in our day. A woman's very eyes wasn't her own, least not as far as the Catholic Church was concerned. Women was told what to see and what not to see. I mind one time being dragged away from the playing pitch at

Thornhead all on account a man who was working in the field beside had no shirt on him. Sister Gabriel—our guardian angel, if you like—had been watching over us from a window in the tower block and come down to rescue us. I still mind the lean muscles on the man and his skin, burned brown as a berry.

I don't think any of these reasons justified the bullying I got but at least I understand why it happened now, and I can forgive Magdalene and her friends. They didn't know what they were doing.

There was times I was that scared I hid in the confessional box. People says a dog smells fear and picks its victims that way. Well, Magdalene and the rest was like dogs in this case. They got wind of my fear and fed on it. Since that time, I hear, them same girls got good jobs in the Civil Service. Bernie Sheedy even become a teacher. But none of them ever left Derry. On a visit back last year I run into Magdalene Cooke coming down Bishop Street. She looked right through me like I was made of glass. She'd forgotten completely who I was. The kind of some people, they prefer to believe the past only happens in history books. Magdalene Cooke's one of these.

For years, I was convinced there was something wrong with me made people pick on me the way they did. (I still get days I think the same, when I can hardly stomach myself.) But whether it only suited me to think this at the time, I can't rightly tell you. One thing's for sure, I never could've taken on Magdalene Cooke and her mates, not even in my mind. I hadn't the ammunition. And I didn't understand or like people very much in them days. Not that I'm fussed on them still, most that I've met. It was easier to blame myself in them days, I suppose. That way I felt in charge, at least, and I had the perfect excuse to go off on my own and not bother my head about nobody.

Getting back to that day in the chapel, "Shamey" was scribbled all over my bag with big curlicues at the beginnings and ends of the letters. I knew the hand right well. It was Bernie Sheedy's. God help us all, but she fancied herself an artist.

My books and even my gabardine was scribbled over the same way. If none of the teachers or nuns ever passed no remark on this, it was for the simple reason they thought this Shamey was someone I'd taken a fancy to. For it was a regular thing for girls and boys, to write the names of people they fancied on their school things. It was expected, you see. It was part of growing up. It was part of the uniform.

I knew somebody had been into my bag that day from the buckle which was loosened one hole from the way I usually kept it. I still shudder to think of the occasion. But it was lunch-time and I wanted my lunch. I was aye hungry in them days. At first sight it seemed nothing was touched. I took my lunch-box out. The second I opened the lid, a sanitary towel sprung out like a Jack-in-the-box and fell at my knees. It was spread with raspberry jam to look like blood. I can still see the seeds, like little eyes, staring up at me off the floor. For fear of being seen, I instantly lifted the towel and put it back in the box. My mind was in a daze. I couldn't cry nor feel anything at all. Punch drunk was a state I come to appreciate in them days.

PE was the next lesson after lunch-time that day. As you can imagine yourself, I was in no state, and asked to be let off. I told Miss Duddy, who took the class, I wasn't at myself. Well! That woman had no manners! Instead of opening her mouth to answer me like any decent body would do, she just shook her head and pointed her finger at the changing room door.

Nobody could ignore her nice hair and long nails that way. Miss Duddy was a right prim wee woman; bought her suits in Austin's and went to the hairdresser every week. Her face was caked with powder and she wore a dash of fuchsia lipstick for a mouth. I mind her that day. She was on top form. "Chest out. Tummy in. Keep those buttocks tight." You talk about embarrassing. That woman didn't know the meaning of the word and she was so pass-remarkable. She dragged me out in front of the whole class and give me a right dressing down for the way I walked. The funny thing was, this Miss Duddy had a soft spot for Magdalene Cooke. Clumsy and coarse as Magdalene was, she never says a blind word to her. And Magdalene had a thing about her too. Plenty days she'd stay in after school for extra classes in "etiquette." That's what Miss Duddy called it anyway.

This day I noticed, while I was talking to Miss Duddy, Magdalene and Mary Healy was keeping a tight eye on me. Their heads was stuck that close the-gether, I figured they must've been cooking something up. The look that was on Magdalene's face! But neither of them breathed a word to me about the towel in the lunch-box. They even let me shower in peace after the class was over. It was while I was putting on my pinafore again I took heed of a letter sticking out of the pocket. The letter was from Magdalene. This wasn't the first of its kind I'd got neither. I never used to open these letters. But this day, whatever got into me, I decided to. I wasn't scared any more. I just wanted to see how much hate I could stir. God forgive me but I was beginning to enjoy myself. As you can guess yourself, the letter was ignorant and smutty, the way teenage young cutties can be ignorant and smutty when they've got nothing better than sex to think about. I'd just finished perusing it when Miss Duddy stuck her head round the dressing room door. She seen the paper in my hand but let on she didn't. Like most of the teachers in the school, she knew as well as she was living what was going on. Still, she never lifted a finger to help me. That day I decided to leave Thornhead for good the first chance I got.

Fridays I helped out in the communion kitchen in Bethel House. It was here the communion bread for the entire diocese was made. (The nuns was real proud on this account.) It was my job to press the hosts from the wafers whenever they were cold and fill them into wee cardboard boxes. There was five hundred bite-size hosts in every box. Between times I'd eat a handful. (As far back as I could mind, there'd been fish for dinner on a Friday night. And I couldn't abide fish.) It give me a thrill as well, gobbling up the hosts like that.

"God'll get you back and make you fat!" Marie Coll says in a loud whisper in my ear. She give me a start for we weren't supposed to be talking at work.

"Then Sister Agnes is bound for eternity in hell," I says.

Poor Sister Agnes! She was heaving a heavy sack of flour on to the table at that very minute and the flesh on her arms was wobbling like blancmange. This started Marie laughing. Now laughing was a nervous habit with Marie, and once she started, she couldn't stop. She laughed till the tears was tripping her. Of course, Sister Agnes heard her. And you should've seen the glare we got! "Brigid Keen," she gowls across at me, "scour them moulds another time. The crosses aren't as clear as they should be." You see, the hosts had to have these wee crosses printed on them.

I'd just dropped the first pan in water when Angie Page burst in the kitchen door. "Bishop Cleary wants to see Brigid Keen right away," says she. She was all excited.

A call to the Bishop's house meant one of two things: a

telling off (which needed a serious sin in the first place for the Bishop to stick his nose in) or an invite to do him a favour. I was pretty sure he didn't want to give me a telling off for I rarely misbehaved myself. You understand, I'm not saying this to credit myself. I just found life easier that way.

The Bishop's house was over the wall-walk on the other side of the boy's dorm. I'd run that hard from the kitchen, I had to stand a minute on the doorstep to catch my breath. Somewhere deep inside the house I heard the doorbell chime. Annie Zachery, the Bishop's housekeeper, answered it. She glowered at me. "You come the wrong way," says she. "You should've gone round the back."

Now Annie Zachery had a name of being a right cross wee woman. And her looks didn't help her reputation none neither, for she had these blue-black lips the colour of death, and blood-shot eyes that darted all over the place. Her hair was like steel wool wound in a knot at the back of her head. And she had this habit of fidgeting with her hands as if she was trying to keep a tight rein on them. Her feet was wild big and noticeable into the bargain. The youngsters used to make fun of her on this account. Not but she asked for it, advertising the fact by wearing Hush Puppies.

I was wondering whether or not she was still wanting me to go round the back of the house.

"As y're here, come in!" she says and steps just far enough out of my road to let me past.

Inside, the walls were festooned with photos of the Bishop shaking hands with this priest and that cardinal. And diplomas! God, but the Bishop must've been a terrible educated man. Then all the clergy is. A life-size statue of the Saint Martin beamed down at me from a stand in the hall. And, at the foot of the stairs to the kitchen, a good-looking picture of Our Lord showed me his bleeding heart. I think I stared, for the heart filled the entire cavity of his chest.

One of Annie's hands shot out to show me the way to the scullery. Once there, she showed me the chair which was deliberately placed there for the purpose of interrogation, I should think. For it faced a tall dresser filled with silver pots and plates and fine-bone china—a kind of high-altar to good housekeeping, if you like. Where Annie ever found occasion to use this much china, I couldn't imagine.

"Next Sunday is the last Sunday in Advent as you know," Annie starts. And she stops again, like she was expecting me to pass some remark on this. But when I says nothing to her, she went on again in the same highfalutin voice. "Bishop Cleary wants to give young Father Mann, who's just ordained, a proper welcome to the parish and he thought next Sunday would do."

Father Mann. I'd heard the name before and tried to place it. I vaguely called to mind a good-looking boy called Peter Mann who'd visited the House—oh, years ago—with a crowd of boys from St Columb's College. They'd come to take part in *Messiah*. Chances were he was the same one for he had that holier than thou look about him even then.

"I need an extra pair of hands," says Annie, and she looked down at her own hands like they had suffered enough and ought to be put out of their misery.

Something in me was reluctant to give an inch to this woman. So I didn't open my mouth another time. But it was more than Annie's crabbed manner that put me off. For at that very same minute, I was come over all funny—the way I always did when I heard tell of somebody becoming a priest or a nun. It was like hearing tell of a death.

11

Annie, the old witch, was eyeing me for all she was worth. The shadows beneath her eyes and the furrows in her brow made you think she never slept. It bothered me, her staring at me like that.

"Well?" says she. God, but she could be wild sharp.

"Whatever you like," says I. I can't say I was looking forward to another run-in with Annie but I seen no reason not to help out the following Sunday. Anyway, I couldn't rightly refuse. Looked at in this light, it'd be a grand opportunity to see inside the whole of the Bishop's house. (I'd only seen a bit.) And I was curious to see if Father Mann was the same Peter Mann I minded from the College. Excited would be too strong a word to describe the way I was feeling. I didn't get excited in them days—the reason being there was nothing much to get excited about. And I didn't look forward to nothing neither. The nuns in the House was aye talking about "looking forward" to Christmas and "looking forward" to Easter. I understood what they were saying, but I couldn't manage to feel what they wanted me to feel. Birthdays, holidays, the day I made my Confirmation, was just the same. I never expected nothing and I never got nothing. Life's better, I think, if you treat it that way.

On my way back along the wall-walk I run into Tim McFaul. I made him out in the half-light. Them days in Derry, it wasn't odd to see people out at night, not like the present day. People's that scared to stick their noses out their own front doors now for fear of getting them blown off. Tim was slouched over the wall and dragging hard on a cigarette. " 'Night, Brigid," says he. He aye had a kind word for me. "You look pleased with y'rsell the-night, Brigid Keen. Where you been?"

"Over to the Bishop's," says I.

"Well you should've been to the pictures with me," says he.

He was aye pulling my leg. "Montgomery Clift was on, in *I Confess*."

I liked Tim. He was dead on, not rough like most of the boys from the House. And he was serious too, without being sober, if you know what I mean. Five years he'd spent in Bethel House, after his ma and da was killed in a road crash. He had an uncle, living in Fahan, who was good to him, but the powers that be wouldn't let the uncle bring Tim and his sisters up on account he wasn't married.

I wasn't one for conversation. People was too much grief. But I always had a word for Tim. Tim's mind, it struck me, was outside the walls—outside the walls of Bethel House and outside the walls of Derry city. I could see it in his face that night, the way he looked out over the Guildhall, and way across the Foyle to Gobnascale in the Waterside. Plenty girls fancied Tim. I mind one mealy mouthed girl kept making big sheep's eyes at him. But then we were all starved for a man to look at in them days at the same time as we were scared stiff of them. At least, I was scared of them, or all except the priests.

This night Tim'd been down to The Picture House in Shipquay Street. God luck to him if the nuns ever found out. He'd have been out on his ear for sure, for the nuns was wild wary of the pictures. The last film we'd been allowed to look at was *The Song of Bernadette*, and they took the whole House to see that. What puzzled me was how Tim could afford to go to the pictures and I asked him as much.

"My uncle comes over from Fahan," he says, "he gives me something into my hand. I know we're supposed to give it to the nuns but, ye know y'rsell, they can be awful tight."

Now Tim would joke the rare time about the nuns, but I never heard him breathe a bad word against them before that night. Something was eating him, I seen, and I asked him to spit it out.

"You know my mother wanted me to be a priest," he says. (This was rare for a start for Tim never used to mention his mother in front of me.) "It's every mother's dream, in Ireland, at least," says he. "She used to come into my room at night and every night it would be the same story, the same question, 'Tim darlin', what are you going to be?' And every night I'd answer her the same way. 'I'm goin' to be a priest, ma.' She'd go away and sleep happy hearing that."

"And are you going to be a priest?" I says to him for I didn't know what else to say to him in the mood he was in.

He lets a big laugh out of him. "What do you think, Brigid?" he says.

I told him the God's honest truth as I seen it. I told him he hadn't the makings.

"Certainly not with this hair," he says and rubs back the oily mess with the insides of his hands. Just the week before he'd got it cut like James Dean. It drew attention to his eyes and made them look big muddied pools after a flood. I asked him again what the matter was for he hadn't given me a straight answer the first time.

"Those lies follow me," says he to me.

I tried to argue with him the best I could. "But you were only a wean at the time," says I. "You says what people wanted you to say. Sometimes we have to do that. Anyway, your mother only wanted the best for you."

"The best!" He nearly eats the face off me. It seemed I'd only made things worse instead of better, for he started into this terrible tirade. "You and millions like you think the sun rises and sets on the clergy," says he. "You have them saints before

14

they're dead in their graves."

I didn't like the sound of this at all, as you can imagine. It wasn't the old Tim I was used listening to. Though, looking back now, I see there was some truth in what he says. Derry people, women in particular, made a wild lot of the clergy—and still do. A Derry man or woman wouldn't pass a priest in the street without a salute.

"You'll see, Brigid. One day you'll see," says he to me. And it was then he suggested we go up and sit in the Cathedral for it was a freezing cold night outside. "What did His Holiness want with you, anyway?" he says to me as soon as we were in the chapel door.

I told him what Mrs Zachery wanted and asked him if he knew anything about this Father Mann.

"Oh aye," says he. "Father Patrick Mann, from the Waterside. The word is he's one of the new breed o' priests."

So it wasn't Peter Mann then, unless I had the name wrong.

"And are you going to wait on him?" Tim says, sour as a lemon.

I'd had my stomach full of him by this time. "I'll do as I please, so I will," says I.

"But you won't." He grinned. "The next thing you'll be telling me you want to be a nun."

In spite of myself, I had to laugh at this.

"Ever noticed their wedding bands, Brigid?" he says. He was on a real roll now. "The very sight of them gives me the creeps. My sisters..." He stops and goes dead quiet for a second. "What worries me is the effect them nuns is having on my sisters."

Being the simpleton I was at that time, you may know I hadn't a notion what he was talking about.

"The Church just stepped in and took us," says he. "Them

nuns and priests conspire the-gether, I know. They can't have weans of their own so they take other people's and make them into little pictures of theirselves."

For sure he was raving now. "Whenever y'r tellin' y'r stories tell them right," I says to him. What was all this fretting about his sisters anyway, I wondered. Other boys who had sisters wasn't getting all worked up about them the same way he was. Honest to God, the way he was carrying on, you'd think he was their father or something. My advice to him was to leave everything in God's hands. Says I, "God will look after yous."

"God!" he gowls. "I don't believe in God!"

Well, you can imagine yourself the effect this announcement had on me. Nobody I knew to be Catholic never said the like of that in front of me before. And I couldn't thole it. But whenever I got up to leave, he dragged me down beside him again. He had that wounded look on him, like the look on a dog's got a hiding it didn't deserve. And I felt all responsible.

"I want out of this place, Brigid," says he. He was groaning by this stage. Now, the Tim I knew never used to moan and groan. "I want my sisters out of here," he says. "It's not the same for you, Brigid Keen. You've been here all your life. All I need is a wee bit of land, like my uncle in Fahan, and a house for us to live in."

Whatever about the rest of it, he was right about one thing. I didn't feel the same way he did. I needed a man-God with a human face to protect me. House nor land nor nothing like that never crossed my mind. And to give credit where credit's due, I seen he understood my dilemma. For he began to renege on what he says before. The old Tim I knew was showing his face again. "Maybe you're right," says he a couple of times. "Maybe God will provide for us in the end."

16

Now it was hard to know what to say to him after this, he seemed that through-other. So I kept my mouth shut for fear of getting him started again. The sadness had come over me in the Bishop's house come over me again and I felt the tears welling behind my eyes though I couldn't say who or what I was crying for this time. I put it down to the night which was one of them still December nights—you know the kind yourself—when, if you believed in ghosts, you'd think it likely to run into one. And you could hear a pin drop inside the Cathedral. Looking back now, I know my silence at that moment put Tim off more than anything I could've said would've done. I was on my high horse and he wasn't going to drag me down off it. Tim would've preferred it, I think, if I'd joked a bit, even flirted with him. If I'd been any of the other girls, he'd likely have tried to kiss me by this time. But he never did try to kiss me, though I had reason to think he fancied me. He had that look in his eye. You know the kind I mean. But I left him there without a word.

By the time I got back to the communion kitchen, my head was spinning. Sister Agnes says to me to keep an eye on the paste in the mixer. It was while I was standing there, watching the paste go round and round, it occurred to me this was a rare way for the Body of Christ to start. I wasn't given to odd thoughts like this as a rule. But that night I was fit for anything. What between Annie Zachery coming over all high and mighty, and Tim carrying on the way he did, I didn't know where I was in the middle of it. I suppose I wasn't used to thinking or feeling much in them days. That's the truth of it. Life inside the House was that quiet generally and I'd grown used to, and liked, the peace inside my head. Then there come times, like this evening, when somebody got me all riled up. God, but I hated that. I wasn't myself at them times. I felt

17

possessed, like them characters you read about in the Bible. I dreaded them visitations like I dreaded my periods. They were that uncomfortable and, it seemed to me at the time, unnecessary.

I didn't see the point in having opinions or feelings where they only got me into trouble. The rare time I ever opened my mouth, I got my head chewed off. (I mind, once, Sister Gabriel was livid when I says to her the convent was depressing.) So I learned to keep my tongue in my teeth. Like the proverb says, "He that keepeth his mouth keepeth his life; but he that openeth wide his lips shall have destruction." As for feelings, I learned to control them the same way for I had a bad temper. God, but I had a bad temper. I mind in particular being mad at Sister Marie-de-Lourdes when she wouldn't let me go up the Fountain during the summer. (Youngsters from Bishop Street and Carlyle Road used to hang about there in the long evenings.) The hate I had in me! You don't want to know about it. I scared myself at times like this, for I couldn't ever forget I had the blood of a killer coursing round my veins. Not but I felt equally guilty after. I even got it into my head that Satan himself would take my soul for as much as wanting to live the way I chose. Of course this guilt was very convenient at the time, for it stopped me doing anything I wanted to do and coming up against the nuns in the process. I had my own ways of curbing bouts of temper. Mainly I'd go off somewhere on my own. Praying helped too, not that I ever managed to put my heart into the words. Still it stopped me thinking and that was the main thing. When the usual Hail Marys and Glory-be-to-the-Fathers didn't work, I'd rhyme them off back to front. Somebody since says to me that that was the way devil worshippers conjured up the devil. I got well practised at that

18

over the years. But mostly, I'd just keep my tongue in my teeth and wait for the moment to pass. Silence was the answer to most problems in the House.

The bouts of temper got rarer as I got older. After a while I couldn't say what I thought or felt any more, or if I thought or felt anything at all. I can safely say I lived a protected life in Bethel House. Of course there was a price to pay in boredom.

The House made me a dreamer. I've never admitted this to another soul before now, not even the priest in Confession. I seemed to sleep during the day and come awake at night, like a vampire. The only problem was the dreams had a bad tendency to get out of hand. I mind a real bleak period when every time my head hit the pillow, I'd see my father—or who I took to be my father—for I hadn't seen the man at the time. He never had the same face twice but I knew him to be my father never-the-same. Pictures, like snap-shots, of my mother's grave plagued me about this time too. I had no peace with them.

Of late I'd been wandering round in the same dreams, night in, night out. My mind was starving for new faces, new places, new notions of who or what I might be—if only in a dream. I'd picked the old dreams to the bone. What few novels was about the House was no use to me neither. All of them was like over rich dishes, too fatty or too foreign for me. I craved something simpler.

Whenever the day come round that I was supposed to help out at the Bishop's house, I went to early Mass so as to have plenty time to get ready after. The sky was bright orange that morning, I mind, and there was a hoar frost on the ground. It was the kind of day aye made me feel dizzy. My lone footsteps echoed across the cobbled courtyard as I made my way to the chapel and I rushed to escape the hot breath was hanging round

19

my face. I felt too alive. My nerves was preying on me. And it was a relief to reach the soft light of the chapel, and the silence. The smell of burning candle wax calmed me down. (I still love that old smell.) And all about the walls the statues of Saint Peter, Saint Joseph and Our Lady was looking down at me. But as I gazed back at them, the aliveness I'd felt earlier in the yard seemed to convey itself to them and I seen in their faces, not the repose I was taught to see, but looks of stifled misery. Take them outside the chapel, I thought to myself, and their cries would fill the city. "I cried out and nobody heard me." These words from Scripture come into my head out of nowhere. It seemed to me the chapel worked on these statues, the same way it worked on me, like a vacuum. It stifled their cries.

I seen right well my mind was going to give me no peace that morning. So I distracted myself by watching the few stragglers that come in after me. They separated off at the bottom of the aisle, the men to the men's seats, the women to the women's. One doddering old man had his head bent that low, I figured he must've committed some terrible sin. He genuflected and crossed himself and shuffled into a back seat. A brazen young woman come in after him and clipped her way up the aisle in stiletto heels. The vestry door opened and the Bishop, who usually says the first Mass on a Sunday, come up on the altar preceded by six altar-boys. All the-gether, they looked like a carriage and six. The altar-boys was the newest recruits in the process of being broken in. Breaking in meant serving at the early Mass for twelve weeks in a row. The smallest boy, at the front, stuck his fist in his mouth to stifle a yawn and the one behind tripped on the carpet when he reached to give him a poke. As soon as they had all filed off to their places at the foot of the altar, the Bishop signed the boy who had tripped to put a light to the Advent candle. The boy lit a taper and began the journey across the altar. Everyone was watching for fear the taper would go out. And half way across the altar, it did. Poor wee boy. He had to go back and start all over again. And all this time, the Bishop just stood there with this terrible forbearing look on his face.

If you've been to Mass enough times, you'll know yourself how you can manage to get through the whole thing without hearing a word. But this wasn't the way with me that day. In the raw state I was in, I heard the Mass as if I was hearing it for the very first time. Everything the Bishop says seemed aimed at me. A "newcomer," a "saviour," was being talked about. The words "come, come" sounded again and again through the prayers. "Service" and "succour" is the words I mind best from the sermon. I mind one line in particular from the Offertory prayers. "All they that wait on Thee shall not be confounded." I even took a hint about what I was supposed to wear. "Let your modesty be known to all men for the Lord is nigh." I was high as a kite, I swear. I'm sure you could tell in my voice. "Let me not be ashamed. We pray that with becoming honour we may prepare for the approaching solemnities." Though I don't think the rest of the congregation shared my enthusiasm. It seemed to me God himself was talking to me, that he approved what I wanted and was going to give it to me. The singing sounded beautiful into the bargain. There was this young fella! God! I thought, in the state I was in, he'd make the very statues weep.

Now it was no accident the Bishop asked me to help out at his house that particular Sunday. (I discovered this later.) He had picked me for a purpose. He was having doubts about young Father Mann, you see. Father Mann had been seen out gallivanting—the Bishop's word, not mine—with a crowd of boys and girls from the Long Tower parish the week-end before. And if, as it seemed, he was a rotten apple, then the Bishop was going to have him out at the start. And what better way to try him out than to throw temptation in his way? I was the bait. The Bishop got me there that Sunday to offer me as a maid. Though I should've cottoned on before I did for it was usually plain girls was picked to be priest's maids, not good-looking ones that was likely to run off and get married.

I looked my best that day, I have to say. The frock I had on was violet, with tiny red roses and a snow-white collar. So as to show off my cheek-bones which was the best thing about my face, I pinned my hair back tight in a purple bow. The nuns never allowed us to keep make-up. So, instead, I rubbed a wee bit of paint I stole from the playroom into my lips and cheeks. Though not so much as would draw attention to me. I didn't want to be noticeable.

Annie Zachery was basting the bird when I walked into the kitchen. (I'd minded to go round the back this time.) "You look done up for a dance," says she, and stared me up and down. She looked ready to devour me. "Have them nuns taught you nothing?"

I pulled up the collar of the frock.

"Still you'll have to do," says she, and she shoved a dirty, old apron into my hand. I could make out gravy and jam and ketchup on it, at least. "It belonged to the cook was here and died, but it'll do you rightly."

The apron was that big, it made me look like a wee girl.

There was six for dinner that day, including the Bishop. Father Mann alone hadn't put in an appearance yet, according to Annie. The rest, knowing what the Bishop was like about time, had come early and was upstairs in the library. The big clock above the kitchen door struck one.

"Run up and see if the Bishop wants his dinner now," says Annie.

My heart was in my mouth for fear. I tugged at the apron to get it off but only managed to get another knot in it.

"You'll do rightly!" Annie scowls and lets her hand fly in the direction of the library. "None o' them up there care a hate what you look like."

I had to search about a bit before I come upon the library. I was scared in the meantime for fear somebody would come on me. And all the time I was trying to get the knots out of the apron. I was that through-other I didn't pay much heed to the place. But I can tell you this much, it was nothing like Bethel House nor the convent neither. (It's since occurred to me there's the same difference between the altar and the nave in most chapels.) It was that swanky. Every place had velvet curtains and chairs with curly legs and Persian rugs. And the door knobs gleamed so hard you could see your face in them; not that you'd ever need to look at your face in them for there was plenty of looking-glasses about. And everywhere was grand and bright as well. It caught the light.

God, but I must've looked the oddest sight standing in the library door that day, for I had a tight hold of my apron at the back to pull it in and my face was beaming with shame. I swear, I would've given my soul for a magic cloak to make me disappear at that very minute. Inside the room was cosy. The Bishop and his priest friends was sitting round smoking and drinking whiskey. One priest on his own frightened me at the best of times. But five the-gether! I couldn't get a word out, try as I might. The five faces stared at me, hoping, I'm sure, I'd do whatever I'd come to do and go away. It's odd the things catches your eye at a time like this. I found myself staring at the Bishop's hairy ankle. A good six inches of one leg was visible above his sock for he'd crossed his legs and thrown himself back in the chair in the affected way he used to do. His belly sagged and his thigh pressed tight against his trouser leg. The Bishop had a bullet-shaped head, with the odd grey hair growing out of it here and there. His eyes, nose and mouth looked all squashed up the-gether. "Well, Brigid?" says he. You wouldn't think by the look of him he had such a beautiful voice. I felt the wee black spots in the middle of his eyes boring right through me and I still couldn't manage to get a word out. "To be slow in words is a woman's best virtue," says he, and he switched on that artificial smile of his. At the same time, he bent his ear a bit, as if to hear me better, the way he had a habit of doing in Confession. I had to speak.

Says I, "Mrs Zachery wants to know if she'll put the dinner out."

He took a hard look at the ground in front of him, to give the impression of terrible concentration. I used the chance to take a quick squint round his friends. There was Father Jack Fraggart, a big, confident man with a watery mouth and large hands. Father Jack, as people knew him, had stretched himself out at his leisure in front of the fire. A large whiskey dangled from one of his hands, while the other crept slowly along the back of the sofa near the neck of young Father Bosco. Father John Bosco, for that was his full name, was a pale, dark slip of a lad with bones that looked too big for his skin. He had these big, beautiful teeth as well. But when he tried to smile I could see the nerves quivering in his face. Father Clerkin, who was seated next to the Bishop, was a right sharp wee man. (You daren't go into one of his masses without a headscarf.) He was prim into the bargain, with polished shoes and a polished face and hands to match. The way his collar cut into his throat made him look awful uncomfortable. The flesh from his chin hung out over the top. Father O'Dowd, the old priest, was sitting apart from the rest. He had taken a hard chair well away from the heat. I never knew Father O'Dowd when he didn't have a dour look on him. This day he had his sour eye on the Bishop, only every so often he'd look down and examine his fingernails. He had lovely fingernails right enough. They were pink and shiny like mother-of-pearl. Fit to say the Rosary on, they were. The Bishop hadn't time to answer me before the doorbell rung.

"That'll be young Father Mann now," he says, in a different voice. "Tell Mrs Zachery to bring the dinner right away."

I was turning on my heel when young Father Mann, as the Bishop referred to him, run into me. I didn't take him for a priest at first for he was wearing grey, not black like the rest of them, and his pullover was covering his collar. He had his coat under his arm and hadn't stopped to take off his bicycle clips. Although I was sure I hadn't set eyes on him before, he felt that familiar. He seemed a soft, sensitive soul.

"Wait!" says he. The word was out of his mouth and he had taken a hold of my apron before I could stop him. "You're in some trouble there. Let me help you."

You can imagine how I felt standing there in front of all them priests while one of them tried to loose my apron string. I wanted the ground to open up and swallow me. He was that close I could smell the toothpaste off him, and aftershave and sweat, and I felt the warmth of his breath on my hands for I was still clutching the apron strings. I looked down at his black head. His hair was long and needed a good comb. When he turned up his face to me, I seen he had these big, sparkling blue eyes. The cycling had brought the colour to his face. He'd just come from the Waterside, where he'd been saying his first Requiem Mass. Though, judging from the smile on his face, he was none the worse for it. He apologised for being late. Words just flowed out of him like water out of a tap and he had this lovely accent. (Maynooth does that, I noticed; takes away all trace of humble beginnings like Baptism takes away the trace of original sin.) Neither the Bishop, nor any of the others, says anything back to him. It was clear the Bishop was fuming.

Father Mann straightened up and tugged that hard on his collar, I thought he was going to pull it off.

"Now, maybe, we can have our dinner," the Bishop says and takes a good, sharp look at me.

"A pretty girl, that," I overheard Father Mann remark as I was going down the stairs to the kitchen. He meant it as a joke, I'm sure, but none of the rest seemed to think it funny for this terrible silence followed.

My job was to clear the table between courses while the housekeeper got the food ready for the next course. I'd been told to start with the Bishop and work my way round to Father Mann who was sitting at the Bishop's right hand. But seeing as I couldn't carry all the dishes in one go, it often happened I had to go back and get Father Mann's plate on its own. Now the Bishop, being in a bad temper anyway, got mad at this and when Father Mann riz to remove his own pudding bowl to save me another journey, the Bishop shoved him back down in his seat. "Let Brigid do it," says he and he glowers at me. "You can manage very well, can't you, Brigid?"

Poor Father Mann. He had no choice but to be waited on whether he liked it or not. When I come back into the dining room with the cheese I noticed nobody was talking to him. The Bishop, mind you, was keeping a sharp eye on him at the same time as he was blethering on to Father Clerkin. They were talking about the recent spate of internments and what the Catholic Church was going to do about them. Father Mann looked that put about. I felt it was all my fault and I was dying to say something to him. Maybe it was only hitting him then, poor soul, he wasn't his own man any more. And it was more than clear by this stage in the dinner that the Bishop didn't like him. It seems (he told me later) his spiritual advisor—I think that's what he was called—in Maynooth and the Bishop was very tight and the spiritual advisor had told the Bishop Father Mann wasn't fit to be a priest. The reason for this was Father Mann had dressed half the seminary up in women's clothes for the cast of *The Pirates of Penzance*.

I was pouring out the tea when the Bishop turned to Father Mann and says, "Patrick, what would you say to Brigid for a maid?"

Well, I didn't know where to look. And Father Mann, God love him, was just as flabbergasted. If you ask me, it never crossed the poor man's mind he'd ever need a maid. But the Bishop was of the old school and thought every priest should have one. This was odd really, if you bear in mind how strict the Catholic Church is about men and women living under the one roof and them not married. But the Bishop had no qualms. Indeed it was him was responsible for hiring out many of the girls from Bethel House.

"That all depends on Brigid," Father Mann says back to the Bishop. And then all the faces turned on me. All, that is but Father Mann's. Poor Father was trying to rescue a Marie biscuit he'd held too long in his tea. He was that confounded.

"Brigid's a woman of few words." The Bishop grinned up at me. "Always a recommendation in my view."

"But are you religious, Brigid?" Father Jack, who'd had more than a few during dinner-time, was trying to take a hand out of me. Sure all of them knew I went to Confession and Communion regular and attended Mass every Sunday. "A woman without religion is like whiskey without soda," says he, "hard to take."

If looks could kill! The Bishop give him such a look as knocked the smirk to the other side of his face. And he would've rammed the words back down his throat, I'm sure, providing he had the know-how. "What do you say, Brigid?" he turns to me again.

What could I say? I was chuffed at being asked. Into the bargain, it was dreadful hard for a Catholic woman to get a decent job in Derry in them days and a roof over your head could be just as hard to find. Here was me being offered the two the-gether on a plate. It would be downright thankless to refuse. And, coming from the House, I felt I owed it to any priest asked me. "Whatever you say," I says to the Bishop. And that's how I come to be Father's maid.

◄○►

CHAPTER TWO

I'll tell you this, the women in the parish was wild about Father. They'd use any excuse under the sun, and make up one if they hadn't got any, just to come running to him. It was no wonder neither, he was that good. I mind as well one woman telling me Father was her only comfort when her own man wouldn't pay her any heed. "He's all interested in me," says she. I'd watch them coming out of his room with these big grins on their faces from ear to ear. And it give Father a lift too, which surprised me no end, for you know yourself what women can be like; always complaining. He'd aye come out from talking to them in a right rearing mood. For a man had taken the vow Father had more women round him than any other man in the parish. He had a way with them, as the saying goes, that many men would've given their right arm for. Maybe it was a sin for me to think of it, but I used to wonder if he ever had a woman before he become a priest. He hadn't any sisters, I knew that much. Just a mother who was dead.

Of course I'm talking about the way he treated other women, not me. He treated me like I was part of the furniture. After that first day, I was lucky if I got the time of day out of him. I blamed the Bishop for this. If I'd blamed Father, I suppose I would've left him there and then. And that wasn't on. It would've been too much for me to thole. For I'd grown attached to him even in the short time I'd known him and in

29

spite of the way he treated me. The kind I am, you see, I find it terrible hard to let go. I hold on to people like grim death. And, anyway, where else was I to go? The nuns would never have me back. Many's a wife finds herself in the self same predicament, I know, from the many stories I heard in the time I was Father's maid.

I'll tell you one man, though, had no time for the women and that was Bishop Cleary. He acted like they were a plague on humanity. The only ones he had any time for was old battle-axes like Annie Zachery or Molly Devenny who used to stand for ages under the Stations of the Cross every Sunday after Mass. Honest to God, she'd stand there like she was in a trance with her nose and chin turned up in the rarest twist and a pair of Rosary beads dangling from her hands. It's not as if she had an angel's face nor nothing. I mind one time I got near hand enough to see, I noticed she had this fuzz of fine white hair growing on her chin just like a beard. And her teeth was terrible yellow. As for good-looking young cutties, Bishop Cleary had no time for them. I seen the way he treated them myself. I mind this one wee girl in particular—an actress she was (though there was little call for her kind in Derry at the time). Sunday after Sunday he'd show her up in front of the whole chapel for not receiving Holy Communion right. The more he scowled the worse the wee girl got till, in the end, she broke down in tears at the altar rail. And him! He went on, like nothing had happened and left her kneeling there. Marie Coll knew the girl, and she swore the Bishop put her off going to Communion for life. Wild horses wouldn't drag her after that, is what Marie says to me. It seems, as well, the wee girl's da fell out with her over the whole business and threw her out in the street. Bishop Cleary had a lot to answer for if you ask me. He wasn't fond of me neither. You only had to see the jaundiced way he looked at me to know that. And he never left off ordering me about the place. For months in the beginning, I swear, he was never out of ours. He'd land in without a word of warning. God forgive me if I'm wrong but I think from the tight eye he kept on Father and me he was trying to catch us out doing something we shouldn't be doing. Can you imagine! Nothing was further from Father's mind. And I could've told the Bishop as much if he'd had the plain face to ask me. He was aye breathing down Father's neck. Honest to God, Father was a right bundle of nerves whenever he was around. He wouldn't open his mouth to speak to me nor look me in the eye for fear the Bishop would take it up the wrong way and make something of it.

Women never went running to Bishop Cleary the way they went running to Father Mann or Father Bosco. For a start, it was a hard job getting past Annie Zachery, the old dragon. Then there's some men that women simply won't take to and the Bishop was one of them. His very looks was enough to put you off. I'm sure none of this went unknown to him. And he let his bad temper out on the poor women instead of trying to improve himself. Nor was it the women alone he give a hard time to. He give Father, and the likes of Father who was good with women, a hard time too. Nobody else was going to have what he didn't have if he could manage it. Father Mann, God love him, come in for more than his fair share of flak. Even when the Bishop wasn't in the house along with us, I swear to God, his beady eyes seemed to be watching us out of the woodwork. I only wish Father had stood up to him, for his own sake if not for mine. For one of the first things the Bishop done as soon as Father and me had settled in was order Father to cut his hair. God, I was raging mad at him, for, like I says before,

Father had a lovely head of hair. Nor was this enough to satisfy the Bishop. The next thing he done was order Father to get rid of the nice blue anorak he used to wear. I'll never forget the first night Father come in wearing black neither. "Did somebody die?" says I to him. He had to do away with his bicycle as well. Within a month—I'm telling no lie—he looked like all the other priests in the parish did. It went to my heart.

But you can't keep a good man down, as the saying goes. Father still had his looks and his way with the women and the Bishop, for all his badness, could do nothing about that. I knew a dozen women in the parish at least had taken a shine to him. But there was one girl in particular. Mary Bosco, her name was. She was Father Bosco's twin sister and the two of them was as alike as two peas. Them and Father had been weans the-gether. Father told me once, when he had a drink in him, it was Mary's brother made him want to be a priest. Mary thought the world of her brother too. You only had to see the way she looked at him to know that. But it wasn't only on account of being Father Bosco's sister that Father had time for Mary. She was one of the finest looking girls in Derry at that time and brainy to boot. She had this long black hair, all the way to her waist, and wore swanky clothes like nobody else in the town had. She bought them in England, people says, for that's where she went to university. Few people went to university from Derry in them days, or, if they did, the furthest they ever went was Queen's. So Mary was special on that account as well.

The first I knew there was anything strange going on was one night in the beginning of Lent. I'd just put Father's dinner down in front of him when there come this sharp knock on the door. It was Mary Bosco and from the scared look on her face I knew something was up. Now Mary had made a habit of calling on Father before this and I put no pass on it on account of who she was. Father aye give her the same time he give anybody else—no more nor no less—till this night when the two of them didn't come out of the study till well after twelve o'clock. They'd been in there four whole hours, whatever they were talking about, and Father's dinner was ruined in the meantime. When I asked him if he wanted anything else he bit the head off me. I swear I never seen him in a temper like that before. He had his fists clenched tight like he was ready for murder. I blamed that Mary Bosco for taking it out of him. It hadn't passed my notice neither that Father didn't speak a word to her in the hall when she was leaving, which was rare for him for he was usually that chirpy with people. He used to say to me he liked to part with people on a good note so as that's the note they'd take home with them. Not that night. Of course, he tried to make out afterwards that everything was dandy but he couldn't fool me.

Shortly after the night I'm telling you about I heard tell Mary was married in England to an Asian fella she went to college with. You may know yourself what people was saying, and if my arithmetic is right there was something to their story for Mary had a wean in August of the same year. I could only suppose it was this that had got Father so riled up, though it's very hard to credit for he was coming up against young cutties who got themselves in the same mess as Mary did all the time. Not but I never breathed a word of this to a living soul and Father never mentioned Mary's name again for a very long time. Still, you had to see the look on his face when anybody breathed her name.

After the scandal had died down, Mary come back to live in Derry. People steered well clear of her, even the people that used to be friendly with her. To be fair I have to say Mary was aye a strange one and nobody, except her brother maybe, knew what to make of her. I suppose we all thought it rare to see a local girl married to a darkie like that. And you couldn't blame us neither. You've got to understand. That kind of thing just wasn't done in them days.

The wear and tear of marriage had taken its toll on Mary, the way it did on most women I seen. Some mornings, when I was on my way to Mass in the Cathedral, I'd see her coming up Fountain Street pushing a pram. She had three weans by this time; two in the pram and one tagging along behind. If he was with her at all, her man (Mennas his name was, though people about knew him simply as the darkie) walked a good three yards in front of her. She'd lopped off her lovely long hair. And many's a day, from the look on her, I'd say she'd slept in her clothes the night before and there was big rings round her eyes. She was about a year back, and had just moved into the Rossville flats when she started calling at our house again. Every three months, regular as clockwork, when she'd had as much as she could take of husband and weans, she'd come and leave it all at Father's door. I could hear her from the kitchen scowling and complaining and crying her heart out. I wondered she had the face to do it. You'd never find me running to Father like that, no matter what was eating me. Father was patient as Job, of course. I suppose it was easy enough so long as he only had to listen to her once in the three months. But then she started calling more regular and at all odd hours of the day and night. This fairly put Father out of his way of going. Now, I never interfered in parish business as a rule. (I didn't dare.) But it was me that says to Father in the end he'd have to get rid of her. Says I to him, he wasn't doing the poor girl any good. She was only getting to depend on him more and more. To tell you the truth, it went to my heart to see him, or any man, taken for granted and used in that way. Some women is that selfish! I was glad in the end I spoke to him for Father looked real relieved. "You're right, Brigid," says he. "There's nothing more I can do for her. She's made her own bed and she'll have to lie in it." Them was his words. The plan was for me to tell her he wasn't in the next time she come to the door. (The kind of Father, he didn't like to say no to people's faces.) "Maybe that way she'll go back and talk to her husband," says he.

Not much chance of that, I says to myself. But that wasn't our business. So I kept my mouth shut. At the same time, you have to understand, Mary had my sympathy. Like many husbands I seen, her man never sat with her at Mass on a Sunday. He'd stay down at the back of the chapel with the other men while her and the weans went up to the front on their own. (Not but Mary liked to be under Father's nose in any case.) This wasn't a good sign, take it from me. You could aye tell the couples was getting on and them that wasn't that way. Mary also looked after the house and the weans on her own while that man of hers spent all night, every night in the billiard hall and all day Saturday in the bookie's. Sometimes I used to see her sitting on her own, in Brook Park, watching the youngsters playing on the swings. I mentioned this to Father one day after I sent her away. "Men have a lot to learn," was all he says.

We hadn't seen the last of Mary, though. When she stopped getting an innings at the house, she took to phoning late at night and she'd stay on the phone for hours, going over the same old rigmarole time and time again. Not that I was listening. I just gathered as much from the way Father was talking back to her. In the end, after I'd been risen out of my bed four nights in a row, I told her not to ring again unless it was an emergency. "But it is an emergency," says she. "My whole life's an emergency." The nerve of her! I had no time for that kind of old chat, 'specially at two o'clock in the morning. So I give her the sharp edge of my tongue. "Father needs his rest," says I. Still she wouldn't take no for an answer and I had to rise Father out of his bed. Anxious types like that get on my nerves. They're that selfish. The worst thing is you have to watch every word you say to them for fear of rubbing them up the wrong way. And God knows what they'll do then, out of downright badness or just to get their own back on you. But I was tired pussy-footing round Mary Bosco the last year or so. I'd had up to my teeth of her. And the next night she called, I give her a good piece of my mind. This seemed to work the trick for she never rung again after that.

It was a relief to Father and me to get back to our old way of going. Father liked his wee bit of peace and quiet, and you couldn't blame him neither if you bear in mind the arguments and upsets he had to put up with during the day. The mess some people's lives was in! And just the same as the present day, it was aye the priest was called in to straighten things out. So, when he come home he didn't want no bother nor upset from me. (Though being on my own all day, I was dying to talk to him. I soon got over that, however.) He liked me to keep the house a particular way and he liked the place to be quiet all the time. This was so people who come to see him would feel at their ease, he says to me. He liked his dinner set down on time as well, in case he was called away. At night he had his wee fixed ways with him that I come to know by heart. He'd go round every room in the house before he went to bed and pull

36

the plugs out of the walls. He had this terrible dread of being burned in his bed, he says to me one time when I forgot to put the fireguard up. Every night he took a bath just the same. I'd hear the water running, just so long. And he'd spend exactly fifteen minutes in there. He filled the water to the self same level— just below the middle—every time. I knew for it was me cleaned the bath out the day after. Then he'd brush his teeth. The sounds was always the same. And when he come out of the bathroom he'd be all dressed up again in his priest's gear as if he'd never taken it off in the first place. He shut the door once for the night and never opened it again except to answer a call.

Once I got into the way of going, I seen just what to do to keep him happy. It was music to my ears the rare time he told me how much he liked me being his maid. I lived for them times. I mind the first time ever. It was the spring of the first year I'd gone to work for him. The reason I mind the time so well is because Tim asked me out the same day. It seems like yesterday now I think back on it. I was out in the back garden, picking some radishes for Father's dinner when Tim appeared out of nowhere. I just looked up and there he was standing over me like the angel Gabriel himself. A word of warning wouldn't have gone amiss for I was up to my elbows in clay and soot from the fire. And my clothes smelled of bleach and cooking fat. That was one of the things I hated most about being Father's maid; all the smells about the house attached themselves to me and there was no getting away from them so long as I was working every day. I used to envy them women come into our house reeking of pricy perfume. Father, too. Never a day went by he didn't smell of Old Spice. A time or two I tried scent myself—cheap stuff Marie Coll give me for Christmas, but I couldn't work up the nerve to wear it, it was that noticeable.

Anyway, I kept a safe distance from Tim that day and went on rooting round for the radishes. The ground was full of worms. Seeing I was a bit squeamish, Tim reached and pulled the radishes out for me; for nothing that crawled in the ground scared him, not even the big red clocks that I'd run a mile from. "Would you like to go to the pictures tomorrow night?" says he to me when he had his head down and I hadn't a chance of seeing his face.

He was aye at me to go to the pictures with him, but he was never that definite before. And he put me in a right quandary I can tell you. "I'll need to check with Father," I says. I didn't have to, really, but that was the first thing come into my head to say.

"I'm not asking you to marry me," says he, "just go to the pictures."

You talk about heedless! This kind of remark didn't help me none. And I could see from the way he was kicking the clay with his heels that he was getting into a real bad temper with me. It seemed no matter what him and me was talking about, no matter how innocent, we aye ended up at loggerheads. Or he'd start laying into somebody else with his tongue like he had a terrible bad habit of doing. The very mention of Father's name is what started him that day. And I had a right mind to tell him where to go there and then, I was that sick of him acting like a spoilt wean. But fighting never got nobody nowhere as Father was aye saying off the altar. So I says to him I'd go to the pictures if he still wanted me to. Knowing him, he was likely sorry he'd asked me by this time. God, but that man was contrary.

The same night I says to Father I needed the evening after off. He was all surprised. Except to go to the shops or to Mass,

38

you see, I never used to leave the house and he got used to me being there any time he wanted me. He quizzed me right, left and centre about where I was going and who I was going with. I could see right well what he was driving at. He wanted to know if I was seeing Tim. God forgive me but I kept him going a while, just for the fun of it. Though I told him in the end I wasn't seeing nobody and had no intention of seeing nobody neither, not so long as I was working for him.

"That's good," says he, "'cause I wouldn't want to lose a good maid." Well, I was walking on air the rest of the day. Nobody never says nothing as nice as that to me before. It was good to feel that needed, 'specially by somebody as clever as Father Mann and somebody that people looked up to as much.

Mind you, it wasn't him alone depended on me. Father Jack was aye asking me over to his house to do this or that for him, the reason being he didn't have a maid most of the time. He went through maids like sliced bread. Whatever was wrong, not one of them ever stayed with him beyond three months. And he was aye complaining he never knew where nothing was. He'd ring me up at all hours of the day and night saying he'd screenged the house for whatever it was he was looking for, and would I come over and find it for him. Or he'd ask me to help him sort the collection envelopes on a Sunday or print the weekly bulletin. To tell you the truth, I think he just wanted the company, for times when I got over to the house he'd've forgotten completely what it was he wanted me to do for him. Father Jack struck me as a terrible lonely soul, not at all like Father Mann who was perfectly content in his own company. You'd think a man like that, with so many people after him all the time, would never be lonely. Not Father Jack. Whatever kind he was, he wasn't content with just anybody. He wanted something off people the parishioners wasn't giving him. For a priest he was a bit odd, if you ask me—the way he drank and the things he used to say. Few people I knew had any time for him and, I hate to say it, but Father Mann was one of them. I'll tell you something now about Father Jack might shock you. He never went to Confession or, at least, according to Marie Coll he didn't. And you know her, she never missed a bar. Having all that weight of sins to carry round with him, it's no wonder Father Jack drank and blethered on to people as much as he did. Marie Coll also says he laced the altar wine with spirits. Not that I could blame him. It must be a terrible job putting Communion in people's mouths. And some of the mouths he had to look into! I know I wouldn't want to do it. Ninety-nine percent of the people I wouldn't touch with a barge-pole. And I'm talking from experience, so you can believe me. I mind the first time ever I had to hold the paten for Father after the altar boy didn't turn up. You get a real idea what people is like, looking into their mouths that way, and you'd need a strong stomach to face most of them. Between sickness telling on their tongues, and rotten breath, it's enough to put you off people for life. So, as I says, I couldn't blame Father Jack if he laced the altar wine. There was another thing about him that was rare for a priest; he aye took heed if you had on a new frock or just got your hair done. And a woman likes that.

Us maids might've had three heads on us as far as the rest of the priests about the place was concerned. Not but the self same men'll take notice of a woman if the situation suits them. Take the matter of Churching. In my day, at least, a woman who'd just had a wean wasn't allowed to step foot inside a chapel door till she'd been churched, though her man was let in. And the same applied at the missions. Women wasn't allowed to go to the men's mission and men wasn't allowed to go to the women's. But, apart from times like these, the most of the priests was just like Bishop Cleary. They either thought they were above paying attention to a woman or they were too wrapped up in their own affairs to take any heed. I mind one time in particular I noticed this. It was the day the Archbishop called to see Bishop Cleary. Any time there was a big do in the Bishop's house, all of us maids was expected to chip in and help with the work. This day nobody says nothing to me till two minutes before I was due to go. Father just walks into the kitchen and says to me I'm needed over at the Bishop's. And there was me, in my old clothes, reeking of cooking fat and God knows what. He didn't even give me time to run a comb through my hair. A man with any sense would've known better than that. And I aye believed he understood a woman. God forgive me, but I was raging mad at him that day. No woman likes to be rushed like that, 'specially when she has somebody important to see. As it happened, I needn't have bothered my head worrying. Annie Zachery, it was, come in for all the attention was going and you couldn't get a worse looking, worse tempered woman if you searched hell with a hook.

I went with Tim to the pictures that night he asked me. Needless to say, it was a real disaster as I predicted it would be, with him and me at one another's throats from beginning to end. He took it into his thick head, whatever was wrong with him, that I wasn't going to like the picture even before it come on. Mind you, he wasn't far wrong. I hadn't much time for cowboys and indians running after one another over acres of barren land. *Rio Grande* the film was, if I mind right. No less than three times during the first half he asked me if I wanted to go home. It got so in the end I thought he wanted rid of me. He can't have been getting much good out of the picture himself, he was that busy grinding popcorn into the floor and ripping the packet to pieces. He says to me after, what did I think of it and I told him the God's honest truth. It's not as if I cared whether the picture was good or bad. That wasn't important to me. All I wanted was an evening out and a bit of company. But he didn't understand that and he wouldn't say a word to me all the way up Shipquay Street. It was obvious something was eating him. Still, I couldn't read minds and he'd have to come clean out with whatever it was before me or anybody else could do anything to help him. As it happened he never did give me the chance to help him. Not that night nor never. He didn't ask me out again neither, which wasn't really a surprise. Except to do the garden, he stopped calling at the house as well. Even at them times he refused to step foot inside the door and I had to take his tea out to the street. The rare thing is, though him and me never seen eye to eye, I missed Tim terrible.

It was shortly after this he went to work as a janitor in the Waterside hospital. That was the place they sent people with TB and I was scared stiff for fear he'd pick it up. It seemed a shocking waste him going to work mopping floors and emptying bed-pans like that, him that could've been anything he wanted to be if only he'd set his mind to it and had some confidence in himself. Then he wasn't the only one with them drawbacks in Derry in them days. All was wrong with Tim was he believed nobody was going to give him a break. If I had money for every time he maintained as much to my face! And his way of dealing with this was to give up on himself before anybody else had a chance to give up on him. Least he had the foreroad of them that way, if not in another.

I used to see him every evening coming up Bishop Street. At

42

six on the dot, he'd come sauntering past the Presbytery on his way back to Bethel House. I could've set the clock by him, I swear. He was over eighteen by this time and should've been out of Bethel House and had his own place by right. But the nuns agreed to let him stay on so long as his sisters was living there. Mind you, it suited them as well, for, if rumours was anything to go by, they took a big swipe out of his wages for it. Marie Coll it was says to me Tim never had two pennies to rub the-gether when the nuns was finished with him. Poor Tim. Some evenings I'd wave to him though he never put no pass on me beyond the rare nod. I mind the sight of him still, with his hands sunk in his pockets and his eyes bent on the ground. He looked all gloom and doom and misery in them days. As the weeks went by, a shifty, hungry look come over him. He minded me wild on a starving dog that had been kicked into the street. Aye, in the back of my mind, I had the notion he'd call into the Presbytery on his way past. But he never did.

Tim was changed. Lost for something solid to hold on to, he went whatever way the wind blew. It wasn't me alone noticed this change neither. Nobody I heard mention his name had a good word on him now beyond the fact he was a steady worker and good gardener, both of which was true enough. He'd earned himself a bad name. When he wasn't having an argument with somebody he kept himself to himself a wild lot. And nobody liked this very much. It made them feel uncomfortable. Like people will do, they took Tim at face value. And you couldn't rightly blame them neither. Looked at this way, he could be terrible sore on them. And they had to get their own back the only way they could, which they did by giving him the cold shoulder. Me, on the other hand, I knew different. I knew there was more to Tim than met the eye and I was determined to have the whole business out with him the first chance I got. Fool that I was, I still believed in my heart he'd pay attention to me and be nice to people instead of rubbing them up the wrong way like he was doing. It was a Sunday, I mind, I run into him in the chapel yard. I was scared stiff. But I come straight out and asked him what was eating him. For all the good it done him or me, I needn't have bothered my head. He got all up in arms like I was attacking him and all because I asked him a simple question. There was just no talking to him. His sole concern then was the same as years before; to find a place for him and his sisters to live. But this was just a grand excuse for running away if you ask me. The truth is Tim didn't want nobody next nor near him, he was that scared. I mind the day it hit me like a ton of bricks he'd never come round. It was the start of winter, for there was no heat and I was out to buy some warm sheets for Father's bed, when I run into him at the Diamond. He was on his way back from The Picture House. "Hello," I says to him but there wasn't a cheep out of him. As usual, he was walking along with his head down paying no heed to nobody. I says his name a second time and still he didn't answer me. Then I reached for him. God! You should've seen the glare I got. From the look on his face you'd swear I'd tried to take the arm off him. Not but I'd noticed the same thing about Tim before. He never liked people touching him. It was all fair and good so long as he was doing the touching. But you didn't dare lay a hand on him or he'd freeze you out like a blizzard. This day he didn't have two words to say to me, just the odd grunt or a yes or no. It's not as if I was being nosy nor nothing. I wasn't. Still, I hung on a bit thinking he'd ask me about the work at the Presbytery. But he didn't. He wasn't interested. And all the time, I felt him pulling away from me. His eyes was looking up the hill where he was heading. He says in the end he had to go which was probably true enough, for, the kind of him, he never left himself time to talk. He took all the work he was paid for and more besides. He even did the gardens for the priests though he had no time for them. Summer nights he'd be out till all hours and, in the winter, he got extra hours packing in the shirt factory. Trying to talk to him was like trying to hit a moving target and it wore out the most determined person in the end. I just wish Tim had sorted himself out and been a bit nicer to the rest of us.

It was at the Waterside hospital Tim met Matty. She was an auxiliary nurse—or that's what she liked to call herself. She was just a cleaner, in fact. I shouldn't have been surprised, I suppose, looking back. All the lads about, once they reached eighteen or nineteen, got married. With no jobs worth doing for Catholic men in the town, the only excitement going was getting a woman and settling down. Not but the women wasn't much different which led to a terrible lot of misery all round. Many of the young couples I seen coming to visit Father looked far from happy. I blamed the lack of jobs, for people will aye get themselves in bother whenever they've nothing better to do. And there was no contraception in them days and single mothers was unheard of except in places like America. Marriage was the only way out of a rut for men and women alike at that time. Tim was no different nor all the rest. I consoled myself with the thought that he might've picked anybody, that Matty was just in the right place at the right time. But there was more to it than this. Matty's da had a bit of land out in the country, you see, and she being an only daughter, was due to come into it. And soon, too, for the old man was at death's door. As you know, Tim aye wanted a bit of land and he was going to get it by hook or by crook. It didn't bother him none that he had to marry Matty in the process.

I mind the first time I set eyes on Matty. I thought she was just like all the other girls Tim amused himself with and that he'd dump her as soon as he was tired with her, for that was Tim's way when it come to women. So I put little pass on her in the beginning. I still had it in my head, you see, that Tim was interested in me and that he'd come to his senses eventually. You can imagine the shock I got then, when I seen him and Matty coming up Bishop Street hand in hand. Tim never held nobody's hand. I'm certain he seen me at the window that day for he shied away. And he couldn't look me in the eye when I run into him in Waterloo Place the following day.

You might well be wondering how all of this affected me. I'll tell you this—and I'm not exaggerating when I say it—I thought the world was come to an end. It wasn't just the fact that Tim had picked Matty that bothered me. This was the first time in my life I seen things wasn't going to go my way and that scared the life out of me. Not that you could've told from looking on, for I went about my work to Father just the same— even there didn't seem any point in it any more. And all the time, I couldn't get Tim out of my head. Father seen none of this no more than nobody else. As much as he ever knew was what I says to him in Confession; that I hated this other woman, mentioning no names, for having what I didn't have. And, just like him, he give me a wee talk, as he called it, about the sin of envy. He says to me I should be happy with what I'd got. Instead of helping any, this only made me madder. Nothing would put it out of my head but that I'd get Tim back. As for how to do it, I hadn't a notion beyond making him even more jealous of Father than he was already. And, as you would imagine, this only drove him further away. The trouble was—I see this much now—I wanted the best of both worlds and I wasn't prepared to settle for one. I should've known better than to expect Tim to pay me any heed after I went to work for Father. I couldn't be Father's maid and married at the same time. Not that anyone ever asked me. There was plenty of men about, right enough. I'd see them at Mass on Sunday. But I wasn't one for socials or dances, and that's where most of the women I knew got asked out.

This brings to mind the time Marie Coll and me went to the Embassy ballroom for a laugh. Marie was maid to Father Bosco at the time. We hardly had our heads in the door of the place, but these two boys from Desmond's factory started to chat us up. Mine had a lovely bony face, like Michael Rennie, and gorgeous thick blonde hair. Everything was going fine until the pair found out we were priests' maids. With that, they went dead quiet and started being all nice to us. Half an hour later, they told us they had to go home. But we seen them in the bar after that. Mine ducked for fear of being caught and the other pretended we weren't there. As things happened, I never did get asked out except that time Tim asked me. And neither did Marie.

If looks was anything to go by, I figured Matty was a good ten years older than Tim, and she was wild fat into the bargain. Her stomach was coming out through her skirt and you could see her brassiere cutting into her chest. She was a big bruiser to put no polish on it. It would be paying her a compliment to call her plain. Her hair was that dried up and yellow coloured you'd swear she washed it in detergent. And her clothes aye looked in need of a good cleaning. I couldn't for the life of me see what Tim seen in her, beyond her thirty acres of land of course. When I think of the girls he could've had—but what's the use in thinking about that now? I have to say, as well, I think Matty bullied him into marrying her. Not but he was ripe for the picking. Tim was looking for somebody to look after him and knock some shape into his life. God love him, he wasn't fit to stand on his own two feet about that time. And then there was his weakness for the women. It's my opinion he tried to cure himself of that by settling down—as if that was ever a cure. And there's many a man'll agree with me, I'm sure.

Matty, the sneak, wheedled her way into the nuns' favour and talked them into letting her stay at the convent so as she could be near Tim. If you ask me, she was scared to let him out of her sight a minute for fear he'd take up with somebody else. She never left the place in the six months before her and him was married. That's how I come to see so much of her. She'd be in and out of the Presbytery on errands for the nuns. Every Saturday night she'd come up with the communion hosts. I knew it was her before I opened the door, she banged on it that hard with her fist. Matty was thick as Drumahoe poundies. But I'll tell you another thing was worse. She was vicious as a sniper. You may be sure I did everything in my power to stay on the right side of her for there was nobody could spread poison like Matty could if she had a mind to.

Her ma was dead, rest her soul, and her da, as I says, wasn't at himself. In the three weeks before the wedding, he was in and out of Altnagelvin hospital with his lungs. So the nuns took on them to make all the arrangements for the reception. Matty's da still had to foot the bill, mind you. And, if my calculations is correct, the nuns made a good, fat profit out of it.

The Mass was to be held in the Cathedral. As luck would have it, the only priest available to say the Mass that day was Father Mann. And you may be sure that didn't please Tim none. He asked round every parish in the diocese to try and get another priest. I had to listen to his complaining coming out of

48

Matty's mouth every Saturday night. The names Father got! She called him a starched coat, a two-faced prig, and mocked the way he says the Litany. I wouldn't have stood for it, not from nobody else, 'specially under Father's own roof. But I wasn't going to fall out with Matty for I couldn't be sure what people would think. What if they put two and two the-gether and got four? And I had enough to worry about without having people wagging their tongues behind my back as well and saying God-knows-what.

Six of us that had been in Bethel House with Tim, me and Marie Coll among them, was asked to the wedding. There was no special reason us six was picked, except to make up a decent number on the groom's side. Matty's side was made up of eighty odd, second cousins and great aunts and uncles included. She had a wild big family.

As you can imagine, it was the last thing I wanted to do, to go to Tim's wedding. But I couldn't see no way out. If I didn't go, Father would only ask me awkward questions and, knowing him and knowing how weak I was at the time, he was likely to wring the truth out of me. And I couldn't bare-faced lie to him, him being a priest and all. The shame of him knowing the truth would've been more than I was able to bear. He'd've thought me a right clown, I knew. And I knew what he would've says to me, too, for I'd heard him say the same thing to other people before me. "There's more fish in the sea," that's what he would've says to me. As if that was likely to help. Tim wasn't a fish.

Nothing would put it out of my head but Tim and Matty would never manage to reach the altar rail. It wasn't just wishful thinking on my part neither. I knew people not far from me was willing to put money on it. And it wouldn't have been the first wedding called off at the last minute. There was a spate of them in the parish about that time. Father says it was a sign of the times, that people wasn't sticking to their vows the way they used to. If you ask me it was all for the better from what I could see. I don't mean no disrespect to Father, but he married many a couple that should never have been the-gether. Every day that passed I expected to hear word Tim and Matty had called it off too. Every time Father stepped foot inside the house from his rounds, I expected to hear the news. The doorbell didn't ring but I thought it was Marie Coll coming to tell me. I'd just about given up a week before the wedding was due when Marie Coll did land right enough and her all out of breath. "Have you heard?" says she.

"Heard what?" says I.

"About Tim and Matty," says she.

So there was a God after all, says I to myself, though I minded not to sound too excited for fear Marie would cotton on. "What about them?" says I, pretending I was busy cleaning the sink at the same time.

Marie rammed her face up against mine and opened her mouth wide the way she always did when she was about to tell you something juicy. "Matty's expecting," says she.

You could've knocked me down with a feather when I heard this.

"And the nuns is all up in arms. Nobody in the House is allowed to breathe a word of it, not a word," says Marie.

I was scared for fear anything was showing in my face.

"Don't look so shocked," says Marie, getting all uppity. "You know the kind of Tim McFaul."

Marie Coll had tried my patience before now, but this time she over-stepped the limit. "What about Tim?" says I, as sharp as a razor.

She discovered her mistake soon enough and didn't dare go on. For Marie was one person knew what it meant to get on the wrong side of me.

I presumed the youngster wasn't Tim's, of course.

"That's just what I says," says Marie.

"So the wedding's off then," says I.

"God love ye, no," says Marie. "But the way things is over at the House, anything's likely. There was real ructions. The nuns had Tim and Matty in. And they brought over my wee priest to sort them out. God love him, he looked worn out when he come back. But you never heard none of this from me," says she, warning me not to tell another soul she mentioned it. "I only got this much from the wee girl keeps the books for the nuns and she was in the room next door at the time." The last she heard, Marie says, the wedding was still on but Tim wasn't speaking to Matty. It was her let the cat out of the bag it seems.

Says I, "She likely did it for badness."

"Aye," Marie agreed with me. "For her and Tim is aye at one another's throats. She likely did it to get her own back on him."

"He'll have to marry her now," says I.

"I wouldn't put it past her to have made the whole thing up," says Marie, "just to get her claws in Tim."

God forgive me but the same thought had crossed my own mind. But I wasn't the kind to say.

"Tim McFaul might be a bit of a lad," Marie says, "but he's a catch of a kind you have to admit."

"What makes you think she made it up?" I says.

"You should've seen her just an hour ago," says Marie. "She had a grin on her from ear to ear as wide as the Foyle. Whatever the nuns says, it run off her like water off a duck's back."

I says to her if she'd seen Tim.

"Aye," says she. "The last I seen of him he was going down Bishop Street dragging his tail between his legs."

This didn't surprise me none. I knew no matter what Tim says to me about the priests and nuns, he still took it terrible hard if they thought bad of him. He embarrassed easy into the bargain. He'd take it hard, I knew, the story getting round the House. Then there was his sisters.

All the next day I tried to fathom what had gotten into Tim—if anything had gotten into him. For I still wasn't sure it was him was to blame for Matty getting pregnant—if she was pregnant. My mind kept coming back to something I'd noticed about the people grew up in the home with him and me. They were divided into two lots; them that desperately wanted weans and them that didn't. The House made you one thing or the other. Now me, I didn't want them. (Least, that's what I told myself.) But Tim? God love him, he thought he could make the world a better place overnight. His plan was to give his youngsters everything he never had.

Stories of one kind or another kept reaching my ears over the next couple of days. (Little passed unknown in the Presbytery.) Some people was saying, like Marie did, that Matty had made the whole thing up. And Dympna told me Matty's da was threatening to kill Tim; him that wasn't able to lift a finger. I put no pass on these stories and determined to find out for myself what was going on. Father could've told me I'm sure, but I couldn't bare-faced ask him for fear he'd fathom the reason why. There was nothing for it but take a run over to the House. Once in the door, I kept my ears open and my eyes peeled. Tim was nowhere to be seen. So I thought I'd tackle Josie, his youngest sister, to see what she could tell me. I figured if anybody knew what was going on, she would, for her and Tim was wild close.

"He's been hunted," says she.

"Hunted?" says I.

"Aye. He had a row with the nuns," she says. "He swore at Sister Marie-de-Lourdes and she give him a terrible row."

This was all news to my ears.

"The Bishop was called in," says Josie, "and he told Tim to get out of the House before he threw him out. He's not allowed back in the door again till he says sorry and goes to Confession."

Fat chance of that, I thought to myself. Tim hadn't been to Confession in years and I didn't see him starting again now. This might still mean the wedding would be called off. So I asked Josie what she thought. Poor Josie. She just shrugged her shoulders and let a big sigh out of her.

"What did Tim say before he left?" says I.

"He never spoke to one of us after the news got out," says she.

I says, "What news?" pretending I didn't know what she was talking about. God forgive me, I shouldn't have done it for the words stuck in the poor girl's throat. Still and all, she managed to get them out in the end. Matty was expecting, she says. "She told some girl she was having a fight with about it—just to win an argument. And to get her own back this girl goes and tells the nuns. Matty just went on bragging about it even after the nuns knew, and the story was round the House in no time. Tim come home from work to an interrogation match. Him and Matty the-gether was marched off to the Mother Superior. The next day, it was, he swore at Sister-Marie-de Lourdes when she told him to go and see Father Mann. Nobody in the House has a good word on him now," says Josie, "and I'm afraid the nuns won't let him in the door again."

I asked her where he was now.

"The last I seen," says she, "he was standing outside in the rain and he hadn't any coat on. They didn't even give him time to get his coat."

Josie knew nothing more. So I figured I'd ply Matty for what she could tell me. I'd brung the wedding present just in case I needed an excuse to talk to her. Matty, as usual, had her hands empty when I come on her. The lazy lump! She didn't even bother to get up when I come in. She was half-sitting, half-lying across the bed with the dourest look on her face you ever seen. "What do you want?" she says.

When I held out the envelope to her she looked at me as if to say, "Is that all?" She didn't even rise to take it from me. So I left it down on the end of the bed.

The same as with Josie, I acted like I didn't know nothing about what had happened. "Is everything all right?" I says. "You don't look too happy."

"He's gone off and left me to them stupid nuns," says she.

Still I didn't let on I knew what she was talking about. And she started telling me the story from her point of view like I hoped she would. According to her, Tim was trying to wheedle his way out of marrying her.

"Never worry," says I. "He'll be back as soon as he's cooled down."

Now it's hard for me to repeat what come out of her sinful mouth after that.

"That dirty, fucking bastard," says she. I couldn't believe my ears. And this in a convent too. She hadn't finished neither, for she went on calling Tim every bad name under the sun and more besides. If the nuns had caught wind of a word of it, she'd have been out on the street in no time. But Matty was fly. She was all pure and mealy mouthed so long as any of them was around. I gathered this much from what she says to me: the wedding was still on and it was her sole aim to make Tim pay as soon as she had him "on her ground," as she put it. "Me da'll see to that," says she.

Poor Tim. I wondered if he knew what he was letting himself in for. It was a real mystery to me why he ever got himself mixed up with a woman like that, a woman was determined to make mincemeat out of him. But Matty wasn't going to provide me with an answer to that one. So I headed back to the Presbytery. And who do you think should be waiting for me when I got back but Tim himself and him with this terrible brow-beaten look on his face. He was sitting on the doorstep with his head down between his knees. Says he to me, he'd been there an hour already and would've stayed the rest of the day if I hadn't turned up whenever I did. I just stared at him. Any other time I would've asked him in straight away. But after what I just heard over at the House I was in a quandary what to do with him. What if the Bishop got wind of it? You could bet your life, I'd be out of a job like a shot. Still, I couldn't very well leave the poor soul sitting on the doorstep. So in the end I asked him to come in. Father wasn't about. And, as luck would have it, he wasn't expected back till late. He'd gone to a wedding down in the Free State—someone had been in Maynooth with him but never done the whole time. I asked Tim where he'd been.

"Around," says he. From the look on him, I'd say he hadn't been to his bed the night before wherever else he was. Then he asked me if he could stay in ours for the night. Well, that put me in a right spot, I can tell you. Father had a strict rule about things like that. He put nobody up. Otherwise he'd have the whole parish staying with him and that would never do. As he himself says to me whenever the subject come up, charity had to stop somewhere. So I says as much to Tim. You should've seen the look I got.

"But I'm not asking your beloved Father Mann," says he, mocking me. "I'm asking you to put me up."

Put up with him more like. The house wasn't mine and I told Tim so.

"Don't put me out, Brigid," says he, changing his tune whenever he seen I could be firm with him. "I've nowhere else to go."

I have to tell you, I had no qualms putting people out before now, no matter how desperate they were. I wasn't running an hotel and Father wasn't the Salvation Army. But try, as I might, I couldn't find it in my heart to throw Tim into the street. It was likely true he had no place else to go. Being the distant kind he was, he didn't make friends easy. And he wasn't a liar whatever else he might've been. Tim didn't have it in him to play on me. Still, it was more than my job was worth to let him stay. I knew right well what Father would say. If word got out, he'd be accused of favouring one person over another and that would never do. His parishioners would never trust him any more. I told Tim all this and, to give him credit, he took me at my word without the usual argument. He says he wasn't going to put me in a spot and got up to go. It was enough to make my heart break.

"Hang on a minute," says I. "There's nothing saying you can't stay here the rest of the day."

His face lit up like a Christmas tree. It was then I noticed Tim had aged terrible in the last year. He was smoking heavier as well; forty a day. This day he was lighting them one off another and his hands was shaking that hard he couldn't hold his tea-cup straight. No wonder he hadn't two pennies to rub the-gether. I'd just turned round from the fire to give him a scone when I seen the big tears running down his face. Now I never seen a grown man cry and I didn't know what to do with him. If he'd been a youngster at least I could've put my arms round him. But that wasn't on. And, to make matters worse, at the very same minute Marie Coll landed in on top of us. Timing was never one of Marie's strong points. Tim, the poor soul, kept his head down for fear she'd see the traces where he'd been crying on his face.

"The smoke in here would blind you," says she and gives Tim a dirty look. I had a right mind to tell her where to go there and then. But I kept my tongue in my teeth. I wasn't going to fall out with nobody over the whole business. There was enough people at one another's throats without me adding to it. And it wasn't as if Tim needed my help neither. He was well able to fend for himself when it come to Marie.

"Aye, you ought to take it up," says he to her, meaning she ought to take up smoking. "It would give you something else to do with your mouth."

"Who's in a bad mood the-day?" says she back to him and I could see her giving his leg a right kick under the table. Marie could be terrible forward.

"Did you want something?" I says to her, trying to get rid of her before either of them says anything more. For I was scared stiff things was getting out of hand.

Marie still kept her eyes on Tim. "I just wanted a pinch of salt for the wee priest's dinner," says she. "I hadn't time to go to the shop."

Hadn't time, my foot! She'd wasted a whole hour gabbing on to me earlier in the morning. The truth is, Marie was a wild scrounge and she was aye after me for something or other. This day, I put the packet of Saxa salt down in front of her hoping she'd take it and leave Tim and me alone. But it was no good. She showed no notion of shifting. One after another she bombarded Tim with questions about him and Matty, so many indeed I couldn't get a word in edgeways. Tim just kept blowing smoke in her face and giving her roundabout answers. In the end I felt that awkward between the pair of them, they were that ill-mannered, I went upstairs to make Father's bed. And I didn't come back down again neither till I heard the back door bang.

"How can you stick that bitch?" says Tim when Marie was gone.

Marie Coll had her faults, God knows, but I wasn't going to stand there and hear him talking about her like that. And I says to him to watch his mouth.

"You pick rare friends," says he.

I could've told him Marie Coll wasn't my friend if I thought it was any of his business. (Not that the Pope himself would've passed inspection in the mood he was in.) The thing is, Tim was jealous of Marie Coll or anybody that come near me, which is why he was so dead set again Father Mann even though he didn't want to have anything to do with me himself. As his own Josie was aye saying, Tim was terrible contrary. He would argue a black crow white and he had an awful lot of spite and fight in him. That day, I'm certain, he would've had it out with God himself, providing God was willing to give him the satisfaction. I wasn't going to argue with him, though. I seen too little of him to spend the wee bit of time we had the-gether fighting. It's a pity more people didn't do the same by him. Then he'd've had nobody to fight with. At the same time, I shouldn't blame other people for taking offence at him. Tim could be terrible selfish, I know. For that same day, he didn't ask me once how I was getting on or how I liked being Father's maid though I was dying to tell him. He just sat there with his face a length long and saying nothing. Not but he livened up a bit as the evening wore on and told me some good yarns about the people at the hospital. He could be lively enough when the subject wasn't a sore one. Him and me wasn't pestered with people calling at the door neither, for Father had given out off the altar the Sunday before that he was due to be away that day. It was nice having the house to ourselves, and rare too. No harm to Father! But I was relieved not having to be on my guard all the time and staying out of his road.

Between intervals it wore round to eleven and still Father hadn't come back from the State. I couldn't mind a night like it. It was bucketing the rain and there was a wild wind coming in from Inishowen. Tim, God love him, was dozing off over the kitchen range. I took the butt out of his hand for fear of him burning himself. As you can imagine I was in swithers what to do with him with the night being as bad as it was. Another half hour, I says to myself. I'll give him another half hour and then I'll send him on his way. I had my hand out to give him a shake when the telephone rung. It was Father on the other end and he says he wouldn't be back that night with the weather. There was wild floods all over the country, he says, and he was going to stay down the country till the following day.

"What he doesn't know won't hurt him," I says to myself as I put the receiver down, and I told Tim to go to bed. I give him a pair of Father's old pyjamas and showed him where Father's room was. We had a spare room right enough but you couldn't stay in it for the damp. As I says, Father never kept people and the spare room was never used except as a store for old junk we

59

hadn't any call for—old books and model armies and the like—that Father had collected over the years and hadn't the heart to part with. (There was nothing of mine there. I come to him with a suitcase.)

I never told a living soul Tim stayed that night and neither did he which surprised me considering how free he was with his tongue when it suited him. A good night's sleep did him the world of good. You would've thought he was a different person in the morning, he was that nice to me. Still he didn't broach the subject of Matty which was hanging like a cloud in the air between us since the day before. I know I was aye one for letting sleeping dogs lie where most people was concerned. But Tim was another matter. So I brought the subject up. I'll tell you now, I would've kept my mouth shut if I'd known what he was going to come out with. Says he, he missed Matty. After I'd just put my job on the line for him. Matty! Matty! Matty was all he would think about. Though I still wasn't convinced he cared an ounce for her. Men is such rare creatures.

"Then there's nothing for it," says I (and I was real cold with him), "but go straight back and do what the Bishop says. Go to Confession," I says. I thought this last suggestion would put him off for sure. But it didn't. And away he went just as Father was coming in the front door. The last I seen he was climbing over the back fence with his breakfast still in his hand.

I never seen Tim a single man after that. Him and Matty was married the following Tuesday. The whole affair was terrible drab. Not that the occasion called for anything more, for him and her looked that miserable. Mind you, those of us from the House that was there knew better than to expect anything more. We knew that anything the nuns had a hand in was likely to turn out a catastrophe. The same old frocks that was used on the rare occasion a girl from the House got married was dragged out this time as well. They must've been twenty years old, at least, they looked that dootsy. The bride's frock was all yellow and there was moth holes in the veil. Tim's sisters was the bridesmaids. And with the looks on them, they deserved far better. But there was no saying a thing like that to the nuns. You'd get this big sermon about wasting money when there was weans dying of hunger in Africa. God luck to the poor dying weans in Africa. They got dragged up any time the nuns needed an excuse for being tight. It takes money to look good and them nuns had us feeling guilty every penny we spent on ourselves. No wonder most of us looked like walking advertisements for Oxfam.

CHAPTER THREE

Father loved God—whatever that means. He just put up with everybody else. (I have to confess now, I don't know what it means to love God. Me, I was just scared of him the way a youngster would be scared of the bogie man.) It maddened me, the way Father would kneel in the chapel, sometimes for hours at a stretch, talking to the air when he hadn't breathed a decent word to me all day. I was jealous of God, that's the truth of it. It's easy to love somebody you don't know, somebody you don't have to live with day in, day out. You can make them anything you want them to be. And that's what Father did with God, if you ask me. The Bible tells us, does it not, that God made man in his own image. But I often thought, listening to Father off the altar, that it was the other way round; that man made God in his own image. For the God Father preached about minded me terrible on himself. Not that that made me any less scared of him—God, I mean.

I'm not saying Father wasn't good to people. Far from it. It's just that he had an extra-big conscience instead of a heart and kept himself to himself a terrible lot. It's like everybody round him was just his tickets to Heaven. And he got all sorts, from women whose weans was tormenting them to men who come to take the pledge as a last resort. One minute he'd be giving advice to a young cutty had got herself into bother and the next he'd be consoling some poor woman had so many youngsters she couldn't cope. But nobody was special enough for him to confide in. Except God, of course. And even God was out of the picture. I doubt Father had it in him to love another human being—he was too scared, in my opinion. Or he just couldn't be bothered. I know what I'm talking about, for many's a man come into our house says to me it's terrible hard work keeping a woman happy.

No number of novenas or prayers to the Blessed Virgin could rid me of the rage I felt at God in the beginning. But I was never more jealous of him than the day Father Green was ordained in our parish. Now this Father Green and Father Mann had been great for years. They'd been to Maynooth at the one time, and you know yourself what priests is like when they've been in the seminary at the one time. They stick the-gether awful tight. It's like the old saying; them that prays the-gether stays the-gether. Only, with priests, it's far worse. They're like soldiers that've been in the trenches the-gether. And, what's more, they won't let anyone else in on it. Well, as I was saying, this Father Green and Father Mann had been great for years. Father Green had up and left Maynooth way back in nineteen-fifty-six, just before he was due to be ordained the first time. The reason was a wee cutty he'd met when he was home on holiday the previous summer. Father Mann told me once when him and me was talking about it that all his class-mates was terrible shocked and bothered at the time. As he put it, "you hate to see a good man go to waste." Not but that wasn't the end of it, for Father Green changed his mind a second time and decided he was going to be a priest after all. This was three years later. The story is he went back the day before he was supposed to be married to the wee girl had enticed him away in the first place. God love the poor wee cutty he left stranded is all I can say. Imagine—with all the

63

preparations made and the dress bought. Her heart must've been broke. A thing like that's enough to make you hate men for life. But to get back to Father Green. He was to be ordained in Derry, for that's where his people was from. And since him and Father Mann was that great, the reception was to be held in our house. It fell my lot, of course, to lay on a big spread. The fuss Father made! I never seen him that het up over anything before. You'd think the Pope himself was coming for his tea. And he kept changing his mind about what he wanted made. One minute it was a sit down tea and the next it was a buffet—is that what you call it? And nothing I suggested was good enough. He had me reading all these rare cookery books full of foreign dishes I couldn't pronounce the names of, let alone recognise half the ingredients was in them. I'll tell you straight—I was raging mad at him. For before that day, he never raised a word against my cooking. He was happy enough with what I made out of my head. But that wasn't good enough for Father Green. Lord no! It had to be something special. It was a special occasion, says Father to me, special on account Father Green "nearly escaped the fold." Them was his words. "Father Green was lost," he says, "and now he was found again." I felt like telling him the poor wee cutty left standing at the altar rails must've felt fair and lost. But I didn't open my mouth for fear I'd get a touch.

The Ordination was late in the day on account some of the Greens had to come from the Republic. So there was a wee do earlier in the house before everybody went to the Cathedral. I mind the first thought crossed my mind the minute Father Green stepped foot inside the door. It wasn't too late for him to pull out yet, says I to myself, if only the right word was whispered in his ear. And all day I kept waiting for this to happen. I figured since he pulled out at the last minute before, he was likely to do the same again this time. To be honest with you, I was hoping he would, if only for the wee bit of a stir it would create. But the more people piled into the house with presents and well wishes, the less chance there seemed to be for the poor man to escape. And Father Mann was egging everybody on, telling them how brave a man Father Green was for "admitting his mistake," as he put it. Between the lot of them, they were determined to make Father Green the fatted calf that day. You'll probably wonder at me talking like this, like a heathen—me that spent my life working for a priest. But the fact is I never got over feeling lousy when I heard tell of anybody becoming a priest or a nun. It was like they had cancer or something.

God love poor Father Green. He appeared anything but a fatted calf that day. He was pale as wallpaper paste and looked like he hadn't kept a bite down in a fortnight. And there were these big black rings round his eyes. The first chance I got him on his own, I told him to sit down before he fell down. I'm sure the friendly word didn't go amiss. Still nobody would leave him alone, though they must've seen, unless they were blind all-the-gether, that he wasn't rightly at himself. They kept buzzing round him like flies and pulling and prodding at him. I don't mean to be scowling, but Father, my own Father Mann, was the worst among them. He wouldn't give the poor man a minute's peace. He made a right trophy out of him, dragging him round the place telling everybody how fine an example he was. You have to understand I thought the world of Father Mann. But he had no business doing that to Father Green, not in the state Father Green was in anyway. You'd think a man with Father's education would've known better. But no.

Between having to put up with this carry-on and the airs some people put on when they took the tea off me, I had a right mind to drop tools and leave. My nerves was that bad, I swear, I could hardly catch my breath. As much as I could do to relieve myself was stick my head out the window every now and again for a breath of fresh air. I was doing this one time when Father Jack walked into the kitchen. Now Father Jack and me was on better terms since I seen there was no real harm in him, only devilment. And our kitchen had become a regular haunt of his for it was the only place he could take a drink in peace. This day he put no pass on me and looked round for the whiskey bottle. I aye left one under the sink, 'specially for him, and hid the rest behind the flour bag.

Father Jack never missed a gathering where there was likely to be drink—or a fight neither. The kind of him, he liked a bit of a fracas and where he didn't find one he was likely to make one for himself. This made me nervous, as you can imagine, when I seen him coming near the place. Still and all, for all his shortcomings and in spite of what some people says about him, I liked Father Jack. I was even glad to see him that day for I was feeling terrible down in the mouth. Father Mann, whatever got into him, was treating me like a right skivvy. He had me sponging one woman's frock where she'd spilled some wine on it, and showing every Tom, Dick and Harry where the toilet was. As if they couldn't find it for themselves. Our house wasn't Paddington Station after all. No more nor me, Father Jack had no time for all this fuss and commotion. "Why don't they just get the job done," says he, "and put the poor lad out of his misery?" Every couple of minutes he'd take a wee saunter into the living room, to keep the Bishop happy, then come back into the kitchen again and blether on to me. For a man, Father Jack was a terrible blether. Most of what he says went in one ear and out the other with me. Not that Father Jack seemed to mind in the least. He was company enough for himself when he had enough drink in him. Now that I think on it, that poor man spent most of his life blethering to his own reflection in the bottom of a glass. This day he was ranting on about how the whole town turned out to welcome him the day he come home from Maynooth fifteen years earlier.

"They made a right spectacle out of me, Brigid," says he. "Me ma, who was travelling back from Maynooth with me, made me drive the car that slow through the crowds. And nothing would do her but I'd keep the car window down. All these hands was grabbing in at me. God, it was wild. They only wanted to shake my hand, I know, but I had this terrible feeling they were going to rip me to bits—the women in particular. And there was these big coloured banners hanging across the road reading, 'Welcome home Father Jack.' People called me Father Jack even in them days. It's like they never took me for a real priest, not then, nor after. Was I glad to get in our front door, I can tell you. But that wasn't the end of it. By my soul, no. Me ma, she says I should go out and give the people a blessing and thank them for coming out to welcome me. I owed them, says she, and they'd be expecting it from me. What could I do? But I didn't have it in me to go out into the street again. So I told me ma I'd give the blessing from the upstairs window. I mind as well, I felt just like the Pope himself appearing over Saint Peter's Square. Though that was one short blessing they got that night, Brigid," says he with a right devilish grin on him. "Not but they wouldn't go away and leave me in peace even then. Some of them hung round till two in the morning letting off fire crackers and roaring in at me."

I says to him he ought to be glad, getting all that attention. Many's a one, says I to him, craves that notice all their living days and goes to the grave without it.

"Don't envy me, Brigid," says he.

It was all well and good for him to speak, says I, him that people looked up to that much.

"So you want notice," says he, making fun of me.

I was sorry I spoke then. So, just to shut him up, I filled his glass to the top. There was enough in it to knock most men out, but not Father Jack. He had the constitution of a horse.

He leaned over the glass and stared into it like he was staring into a magic ball. "The meek shall inherit the Kingdom of Heaven," says he in a mocking voice. None of the other priests ever mocked about religious things the way he did. But I put this down to the drink in Father Jack's case.

I picked up the plate of sandwiches I'd been making all the time he was running off at the mouth.

"Let me give you a hand, Brigid," he says. And just as I was passing him, he grabbed a hold of the plate. He tugged it that hard some of the sandwiches fell off on the floor. Give me a hand! He could hardly stand up straight let alone hand the sandwiches round. The job I had talking him out of it; him being the big man he was, and that determined. My life wouldn't have been worth living if the Bishop caught sight of him. Sure as I was living, the blame would be laid at my door. Bishop Cleary would blame me for putting him up to it. Or he'd make out to Father Mann I wasn't doing my job right. The only way I could get him to stay put in the end was to pour him another glassful of whiskey. This was sure to work for he was like a wean with a bottle. Still and all he wouldn't let me go and clung on hard to me like a spoiled youngster. "I wish you'd come to work for me, Brigid," he says. "Why should Pat Mann have the best maid around?"

As I says to you before, he couldn't hold on to a maid himself, though I can't tell you why. Marie Coll told me all kinds of stories but I wouldn't like to say. Marie had a bad mouth on her if she didn't like a person. And she had no time for Father Jack—not since he told her she should've gone to work for *The Telegraph*.

"And what would Father Mann do then?" says I to him.

"Oh, he'd get somebody else no bother," says he. "A pair of hands is all he needs." And Father Jack put his own two hands the-gether, like he was praying. "Father Mann doesn't deserve a woman like you, Brigid," he says.

I'd just managed to get past when Father Green appeared in the kitchen door looking the worse for the wear. (God luck to me, I didn't know where I was between the lot of them that day.) From the desperate look was on Father Green's face, you'd think there was a gunman after him. "Is there another way out of here?" says he to me, looking round at the same time for the back door. Father Jack let a big laugh out of him. "Have the bloodsuckers got the better of you?" says he. Poor Father Green's jaw dropped and he looked at me for permission to go through the kitchen. A couple of minutes after, I looked out the window to see if there was any sign of him. And there he was standing behind some rose-bushes in the garden. Judging by the sounds coming from the outer room, I figured nobody had noticed him missing yet. So I took advantage of the quiet minute to have a word with him and left Father Jack to hold the fort. Maybe it wasn't my place to say anything now I think on it. Father was aye warning me not to stick my nose into parish affairs. Of course he didn't put it that way but that's what he meant all the same. Tea's as much as I was expected to provide and a sympathetic ear if somebody was wanting it. That day, though, I was in no mood to heed anything Father Mann says to me. God love poor Father Green. The sweat was pouring off him in buckets when I come on him and he was fidgeting terrible with a pair of Rosary beads he had knotted round his fingers.

"Does the crowd bother you?" says I to him. I knew right well the crowd had nothing to do with what was wrong with him but I just says this to start a conversation. He didn't look too sure whether to speak to me or not in the beginning which was natural enough, I suppose, seeing as I was a complete stranger to him and he had hordes of family and friends inside the house. But, as you know yourself, strangers is often the only people a body can talk to when nobody else understands. So I just stood there and let him take his time. Mind you, I was scared stiff with every second that passed for fear Father Mann would come along. And I didn't like to think what Father Jack might be up to in the kitchen. I was just about to give up when Father Green finally decided to open his mouth.

"I'm afraid to go through with it," says he. This wasn't news to me, of course, though I didn't expect to hear him come out straight with it like that. And he had these big tears in his eyes. I didn't know for the life of me what to say to him. I must've looked a right stoodgy, standing there with my mouth open. "All those people in there are expecting it of me," says he. "They think I'm cut out for it as my mother used to say. But I never felt less fit to be a priest than I do today."

"There's still time to pull out," says I, blurting out the first thing come into my head. It was only after I says it, I realised this was the last thing he wanted to hear. He didn't need me adding to his confusion. And I seen him thinking, "it's easy for her to talk," though he didn't say nothing. He just looked at me real suspicious like I might be the devil in disguise. My insides shrunk.

"You know," says he, "I envy priests like Father Mann. They know what they want. They're sure of themselves."

With that I heard the sounds of raised voices coming out the kitchen door. The leeches was on to him and they were coming out, the whole throng of them, to drag him in. Poor creature! He shrunk further behind the rose bushes in the hope nobody had seen him. But it was no good. They'd spotted him already. When I looked back I seen Father Mann leading a string of them across the lawn.

"You can always tell them it's called off," I says to Father Green, keeping my voice down for fear anyone else would hear me. Can you imagine what Father Mann would've says to me if he heard me talking in that way? It might even be a sin, I thought to myself. If so, I'd have to tell him in Confession whether I liked to or not. Then, what would he say? Me tempting a priest away from his vocation like that, and under his roof too. Not to mention the priest in question being a friend of his. I was that anxious for a second, I forgot Father Green. Not but he wasn't caring. He was talking on just the same. His eyes was far away and he was paying no heed to the approaching tribe. Something had happened him for his voice was clearer.

"I don't care that other people expect it of me," says he. Now this was changing his tune from a minute ago. "The real trouble is," says he, "I expect it of myself. Ever since I was a boy I wanted to be a priest. And the notion still won't let me be."

It was then, for the first time, I had any inkling what it meant to "have a vocation." And I wondered if Father Mann grew up feeling the same way. If he did, I says to myself, then I had no business being mad at him. Maybe he had no choice like poor Father Green was just describing. And here was me raging at him the whole time and all on account he wouldn't pay me any heed. But, speak of the devil! That same second he barged right past me like I was invisible. He threw his arm round Father Green's neck and whispered something in his ear. I couldn't make out what it was he says though, for I was trying to get my balance straight. Then he says in an exaggerated voice, so as everyone could hear, "They're waiting on you inside, Michael." And he grinned a big broad grin to cover over any trace of trouble Father Green might've left. All this time he hadn't as much as looked at me. But you should've seen the glare I got when everybody else's backs was turned. If looks could kill, I'd be six feet under. I have to tell you this; the guilt I'd been feeling earlier, about wanting that man's attention just disappeared, and I was raging mad at him again. Priest or no priest, I says to myself, nothing give him the right to ride rough-shod over people's feelings the way he just did.

God love poor Father Green. Whether he liked it or not, he was dragged back into the house. I could see no hope for him now, not with a mob like them inside after his blood and him being the quiet soul he was. Sally Green, his sister-in-law, who was still hanging round after the others went in, looked me up and down as much as to say I had no business being there and me in my own garden. Women like that, with notions about themselves, just gets on my nerves. May God forgive me, but I couldn't help smiling to myself when I seen her catch her new frock in a whin bush. Of course, Father Mann signed me from the kitchen window to give her a hand. But I pretended I didn't see him and left her there to get herself out of the tangle she was in.

The Ordination Mass was the first of its kind I'd ever been to. For weeks before, everyone who come into our house was talking about it. The whole parish was excited. So I thought I ought to be excited too. It just goes to show you how easy it is to get taken in when there's enough people round wanting to think the one way. The women who did the altar was having a real field-day. A speck of dust wasn't safe round them women at any time. But they virtually camped out in the chapel that week. And they were over in ours every whip about, looking for one thing or another; shampoo for the carpet, as if the carpet wasn't clean enough, and wax for the altar rail. And they had Father over inspecting the flower display three times the day before the ceremony. Everybody could manage it was trying to get in on the act. Men was queued from our house to the Cathedral when Father asked for stewards and the choir was practising every night.

I'll tell you this now. That Ordination was the worst performance I ever sat through in my life. For a start, the place was that cram-packed you couldn't move an elbow. And it was terrible warm. People was falling out the door and the chapel yard was full. Everybody was able, and some that wasn't, had come out to see the boy who did good for himself. To them people's way of thinking, nothing compared with being a priest. A loud speaker was set up outside so as the people in the chapel yard could hear. Marie Coll and me was lucky, though. A friend of Marie's kept us two seats in the balcony so we could see everything was going on. Father Green's people was all dressed up to the ninety-nines—the women in hats and the men in suits and ties. You'd think, by the style of them, it was a wedding they were coming to.

Time was getting on. It went way past three o'clock, the

time the Mass was supposed to start, and still nobody appeared on the altar. And there was no sign nobody was going to. The congregation was getting terrible restless and the youngsters, who had no call being there in the first place, was shifting round in their seats. Then one whisper started another and another until the chapel was full of voices. Carry-on like this is all well and good in a bingo hall, but it's downright disrespectful in a chapel, if you ask me. And I glared at anybody near me that dared to open their mouth. May God forgive me, but I think I'd had it with my nerves that day.

The Guildhall clock struck half past three by which time Mrs Green couldn't contain herself a minute longer. In spite of her husband's brave efforts to keep her in her seat, she up and pranced right into the sacristy. She didn't genuflect or as much as cross herself neither when she was passing the Tabernacle. The people went dead quiet. All eyes was turned to the sacristy door to see what was going to happen next. After only a minute Mrs Green come out again looking far from happy. She was gripping her handbag tight against her chest and her face was all screwed up like she'd just eaten a bite out of something sour. (Marie Coll told me after what had happened. Father Green, it seems, had fainted in the sacristy and Mrs Green was mad at him.) She come down to her seat. But would she sit down? Lord, no. Instead, she started into her husband like he was to blame for everything. I didn't hear nothing her and him says, of course. But I only had to see the way they glowered at one another to know they were at loggerheads. She was still laying down the law when the sacristy opened and the procession come out. Bishop Cleary, who was wearing a big grin on his face for some reason, was at the front and Father Green was dragging his feet along at the back. In between was a whole string of priests, Father Mann among them, whose job it was to serve Mass. This was the way on special occasions like the-day; the priests was expected to do the jobs of altar boys.

It must've been terrible sore on Father Green—all them hundreds of people staring at him, not to mention the Bishop breathing down his neck. And him, poor man, not at himself. The time he was flat out on the ground, I swear, I didn't think he had it in him to rise again. But Father Jack, God love him, give him a helping hand. I don't see the need for all that carry-on, to be honest with you. Being a priest is just a job like any other job. And I don't understand why priests can't just get documents to say they're priests the same way doctors and lawyers can.

As soon as the Ordination was over, Father Green went into the sacristy and come back out a couple of minutes after in all the gear. The congregation was waiting on him in the meantime, the way wedding guests would wait for a new bride to appear in her going-away outfit. He had on these split new vestments, real fancy ones, like none of the other priests in the parish had. They were a present, it seems, from an uncle of his in America who was well off and could afford that kind of thing. But pricy or not, Father Green looked far from comfortable in them. He kept shifting the tunicle off his shoulders like it weighed too heavy. And the surplice needed a good turning up.

People make a whole lot out of a priest's first Mass. The sermon, though, is what they really come for. From that they judge what a new priest is going to be like; whether he's going to give them a hard time or not. The people that come to see Father Green went away with heavy hearts that day, I dare say, for he went on about nothing but the "great demands" God placed on us. "We must die to ourselves before we can come alive in the Lord"—them was his words. You have to admit yourself, this was a dreary thought for a first sermon, 'specially coming from a man as young as he was. And he sounded terrible weary and down in the mouth into the bargain. All the time I was listening to him, I couldn't help but think of the way he looked in the garden earlier in the day.

The kind of Marie Coll, she couldn't stay at peace a minute. She was fidgeting round in her seat that much in the end she was getting on my nerves, and I glared at her for all I was worth. Not that it did any good for Marie had skin as thick as leather. She nudged me in the ribs and drew my notice to a girl was sitting a couple of rows away from us. "It's the one he was going to marry," says she in my ear.

"Whisht," says I, for I was scared stiff anybody else would hear her. Then I took a look at the girl for I was curious myself to know what kind of woman could entice a man away from being a priest. But there was nothing special about her as far as I could make out. She was dead ordinary; ordinary face, ordinary hair, ordinary clothes. It's like they say. There's no accounting for taste. I was surprised she was there at all under the circumstances. Like me, maybe she was waiting for Father Green to change his mind at the last minute and wanted to be there to stake her claim whenever he did. Or maybe she was a glutton for punishment. She looked dead miserable, right enough, like she'd just been jilted the day before. And there was no man with her, least none that was sitting beside her anyway. Some women is like that, give everything they've got to some no-good man that doesn't want them. Then spend the rest of their lives being miserable and letting their anger out on other people instead of getting on with their lives like they should be doing. I have to admit, I found it hard to keep my eyes off this one the rest of the Mass for fear I'd miss something.

Come the time for Communion, she wouldn't stop staring at people coming down from the altar rail. Men and women alike. And she had this real spiteful look in her eye. It's like she was jealous of anybody that as much as went near her Father Green. She waited till the very end to go up herself. (Me, I wasn't going. I couldn't be bothered with the crush. So I had ample opportunity to keep an eye on her.) Father Green didn't notice her till she was kneeling there in front of him. But the second he seen her, he froze like a statue. Father Mann, who was carrying the paten for him, had to give him a nudge to carry on. And even then he was all in one piece with shock and embarrassment. It was terrible embarrassing to watch into the bargain. Poor man. He was in that big a fluster he couldn't get a host out of the chalice. I know myself, from working with the hosts in the communion kitchen, the way they stick the-gether. It needs a steady hand to take them apart. And Father Green hadn't a steady hand that day, God love him. Marie Coll, who like I says, never missed nothing, give me another good hard nudge and started to snigger. It wasn't us alone was staring neither. The whole chapel was watching the proceedings by this stage. As if it wasn't enough that Father Green couldn't get the host out of the chalice; whenever he did manage to get it out and tried to put it in the girl's mouth, he dropped it. There was the usual fuss while the spoiled host was carried off to the sacristy. And all this time the girl just knelt there. I wonder she had the gumption, knowing what people was likely to say about her. Whether she meant to or not, she won a real coup that day. She managed to mess up Father Green's first Mass as only she had the power to do. Not but the poor man tried to go on

77

afterwards like nothing had happened. And I seen Father Mann scowling the girl behind the Cathedral when the Mass was done.

Father Green never spoke another word to me that day or for months after. And he went red in the face any time I run into him in the town. Many's a time, indeed, I seen him go out of his way whenever he seen me coming. Not that I blamed him, poor soul. He was likely ashamed about giving himself away to me the way he did. I know the feeling myself. There's many a thing I've said I'd like to take back. That not being possible, I'm now more careful than ever to keep my mouth shut.

At the reception in the evening, Father Jack was in terrible low spirits which was a rare thing for him considering there was plenty drink flowing. People aye relied on him to be the life and soul of the party. So when speeches was called for, I wondered what he was going to say for I'd heard nothing but groaning and complaining out of him ever since he come back from the Cathedral. The Bishop, being the guest of honour, got up to speak first. Well you never heard such empty drivel in all your life. Like some politicians I heard on TV, the Bishop had this knack of talking for ages and saying nothing at all while at the same time saying all the right things, all the nice things he was supposed to say. The audience clapped and cheered for him. But, if my life depended on it, I couldn't hardly mind a single word he says after he was finished. Mr Green, Father Green's da, got up to speak next, though it took a whole lot of coaxing to get him to agree. He was scared, you see, of making too much of "his boy," as he called him. At the same time the pride he felt shone through in every word he says. He told how himself and Mrs Green never pushed Michael to be a priest. Says he, they knew it was a terrible hard road for any young man, 'specially in that day and age. (It was the Sixties by this time.) Michael, he says, had aye been the one to remember the Rosary at night. "He never had to be forced to Mass or Confession like many a youngster," says Mr Green. Now, no harm to the old man, but this kind of talk made me sick. It come Father Jack's turn to say something after him. You should've seen the look on Bishop Cleary's face when Father Jack stood up with the whiskey glass still in his hand.

"Brethren," says Father Jack with a kind of grin on his face that made him look like he was in agony. He was brushing aside the need for niceties with a broad sweep of his hand when he spilled some of the whiskey. "If this was altar wine," he says with a laugh, "we'd have a right handlin', wouldn't we?" And he looked straight at Father Green.

It took no brains to see he was harping back to the accident with the Communion host. Poor Father Green looked like he was going to die with shame.

"But as it is," says Father Jack and looks at me, "Brigid here can clean it up. Can't you, Brigid?"

Well, everybody turned and looked at me. You'd think from their faces it was my fault Father Jack mentioned my name. They glared at me like I had no business being there and me in my own house. Not but they got what they wanted for I run off to the kitchen. Wild horses wouldn't drag me back into the living room after that. Marie Coll, God love her, let the vultures out and I had to put up with them no more.

But the minute the last person was gone, I heard Father's footsteps coming towards me. The house felt terrible big and empty at that minute, and I was scared out of my wits. Father was never one for biding his time when something was eating him. Me, on the other hand, I just sat there and kept my tongue in my teeth for I knew what was coming before he opened his mouth. And I didn't have words to describe what I was feeling or the presence of mind to argue with him. He started the way he always started, by praising me. This never fooled me none, though. I knew the only reason he did this was to ease his own conscience and give the impression of being fair with me. Nothing hid the fact he was all riled up and dying to have a go at me, whatever was eating him. I had a wild hard job fighting back the tears, like any time he give me a touch.

"You should've been at the door to see the people out," says he. "That's your job. That's what I pay you for."

Pay! I hadn't had a penny off him in the past six months. The way things were, you see, I didn't get regular wages, only my bed and board and whatever odd shilling himself or the Bishop pushed my way. Not that I ever I wanted for anything. I'm not complaining. But it would've been nice to have some money to myself now and again.

"I'm sorry," says I.

"Whatever got into you?" says he.

God, he could be wild thick sometimes. Anybody with any sense would've seen the way them people was treating me and understood my anger. But I was in no mood to explain myself to him. I was too tired. And, anyway, I knew he wouldn't understand. He'd just tell me I should've stood my ground. It was all well and fine for him to think like that. He was a man and people looked up to him.

"But that's not really what I'm bothered about," says he when he seen he wasn't going to get an answer out of me why I hadn't let his visitors out. "You had no business keeping Father Green in the garden this afternoon when he had a houseful of guests to attend to."

Now that was typical of him, accusing me of putting in on Father Green when things was the other way round, if anything. Not that I minded listening to the poor man. I'm not saying that. I was trying to figure out a way to explain what had really happened without talking behind Father Green's back. But I didn't have the time.

"It's no matter now," says he. "What's done is done."

Now, I did a lot of thinking about everything had happened that afternoon. And, let me tell you, there was a lot more going on here than met the eye. Father didn't like me talking to people, whatever the reason. I don't know how I knew this but I knew it. I couldn't speak to another person or as much as look sideways at them without him getting all het up. It's not that he wanted me to talk to him instead. Far from it, in fact. He just liked to have everything around him under control, and that included me.

I mind, in particular, the morning after Tim stayed at our house for the night. Of course I didn't tell Father he'd stayed, just that he'd come in for a bite of breakfast in the morning. Well, the look I got! You'd think I'd been entertaining the devil himself. I seen Father's eyes light on the remains of the fry Tim had left behind him. God forgive him, but I think he begrudged the poor soul even that. And him knew right well Tim hadn't had a roof over his head or a decent meal in days and all on account he was being hunted from pillar to post by nuns and priests. But it wasn't Tim alone made Father angry. He didn't like to see me talking to any man—not even one I run into in the chapel yard. He was afraid they'd tempt me away from being a priest's maid. And being a priest's maid was best next thing to being a nun in his opinion. I reckon he figured, so long as I was in God's pocket, I was in his pocket as well.

81

I says he didn't like Tim. Well, he didn't like Dympna neither. There was a terrible bad atmosphere in the house so long as she was there and he was around. And, after she went away, he'd quiz me right, left and centre to find out what she wanted off me. He was that scared for fear she'd turn me against him. God! You'd think I didn't have a mind of my own the way he was going on. It got in the end I dreaded anybody coming to the back door to see me. (People that come to visit me wasn't allowed to use the front door.) There was no joy in having people in the house. Of course he was aye telling me to invite whoever I liked. He even says I could use the drawing room if I wanted. But when it come down to it, he didn't like any of the people I brung in. Not that he ever says nothing to their faces, mind you, or to me neither. I supposed he couldn't, being a priest and all. Still, I knew what he was thinking even when he didn't say nothing. He just left me with this real bad feeling which wasn't helped by the fact I couldn't talk about it. This was another way he had of keeping me in my place; not to speak his mind, I mean. And he willed me—that's the only way I can put it—to do the same. That way I couldn't make no inroads on him and he didn't have to argue with me. That would've taken too much out of him and he didn't hire me to take it out of him. The one visitor I had that he could abide was Marie Coll. Then that was only on account she was Father Bosco's maid.

There was another reason why Father didn't like people taking an interest in me. He was afraid I'd get notions about myself and, knowing me, he was probably right. I could be wild big-headed and full of myself at times. Take, for instance, the time I got talked into an outing with the teachers from the Long Tower primary school. There was this one among them, Joy Close her name was. Well, this Joy stuck to me like a shadow and we talked all the way to Bundoran and back. She knew a terrible lot about the nuns in Bethel House and was able to tell me all about their people. (It was aye a sore spot with me when I was growing up that none of them give anything away.) But that's not the only reason Joy and me hit it off. When she heard I'd come from Bethel House she wanted to know what it was like to be brung up by the nuns and she asked me all kinds of questions about myself. I was high as a kite when I arrived back at the Presbytery that night. But I wasn't five minutes in the door before I started getting depressed again. Father was going about his business as usual and didn't take the least bit notice of me, which felt rare in the wake of Joy being that interested in me. Into the bargain, that same night young Father McLaughlin who'd just come to work at the College come into ours and Father had all the time in the world for him. Then he always had time for people was educated. He'd spend hours talking to them when he hadn't a word to say to me. It used to make me wild mad.

I might as well have talked to a brick wall as try to talk to him that evening of Father Green's Ordination. Not but in the mood I was in, I didn't think he was worth the bother after the way he treated me, to say nothing of poor Father Green or Father Jack, for he wasn't very nice to them neither. So I kept my tongue in my teeth. But I know what you're thinking; that I just did this to avoid an argument. And you might be right. I'd be the first to admit, I never was good at holding my own with words. Many's a time I seen other people argue like cats and dogs and come out of it with flying colours. Not me. I'd be in a wild way for days if somebody as much as looked sideways at me. And I'd be terrible confused. I couldn't tell if what I thought or felt was right or wrong any more. And I was that scared in the end I couldn't open my mouth even it was to save my life. And this time was no exception. I couldn't tell if I'd done the right thing talking to Father Green or not. Maybe the devil had got a hold of me after all. Or maybe, as some people seemed to think, I didn't have a proper respect for the clergy.

There's no denying, though, Father himself was in a rare way that day, whatever got into him. I never seen him in the same temper before nor after. And if you want my opinion what was happening, he was letting out his bad feelings on me. He was trying to prove to himself, or whoever else was interested, that he had no call for women the same way Father Green had no call for them. And it bothered him when he seen Father Green needed somebody to talk. For as far as he was concerned, priests didn't need nobody except God, which is a whole lot of nonsense if you ask me. Doctors and lawyers spend their whole lives attending people the same way a priest does, but there's no rule saying they can't get married if they want to.

Now there was one face at the Ordination I haven't mentioned so far. That was Mary Bosco. And the reason I says nothing about her before is I wanted to give her a bit of space to herself. For I've been sore on her in the past and I think I owe it to her. You may know, it was a real shock for me to see her there at all considering the way Father and me had treated her. Then people might've noticed if she wasn't invited (her being Father Bosco's sister and all) and made something of it. I had to admire the way Father ignored her the whole day, except to be civil to her. And, right enough, she behaved herself. It was only afterwards the trouble started. I know I says I'd be fair to her but, honest to God, that girl had no shame in her. Once she got an innings that day, she didn't leave off pestering us for weeks after. She turned up on the doorstep every night, regular as clockwork. Of course I did what Father ordered me to do in the beginning and told her he wasn't there. And, I'll tell you this, I didn't have no pangs of guilt neither. What business had she putting in on Father every night of the week? It was too much to expect, even of a priest. Not another soul in the parish ever dared put in on Father the same way. Not to mention the fact she had three youngsters and a husband to look after at home. A woman like that had no business sitting in our hall half the day, waiting to catch Father on the off-chance. It maddens me at any time to see people that wrapped up in themselves, they've no time or consideration for the rest of the world. Anyway, that's what I was thinking about Mary Bosco before I heard the whole story.

Things might've been all right if she'd confined her attentions to Father and left me well enough alone. I don't know what she wanted with me anyway; sure I was a good ten years younger than her. I was willing to give her a cup of tea, the same as I'd do for anybody that come in to see Father. But, one cup wasn't enough for Mary. Lord, no! She had to have another and another, and she'd sit there, for hours, smoking me out of house and home. That was another thing I couldn't stand about her. She smoked like a trooper, the same as Tim did. Leaving aside the fact I couldn't stand to see a woman with a fag dangling from her mouth, my chest got that sore in the end, I had to tell her to stop or take her smoke into the garden. And, right enough, she did what I told her without a murmur of complaint. It was this quietness in her struck me as rare in the beginning; for Mary had a name of being argumentative, not to mention uppity, on account of who she was. But I put no more pass on it at the time. And she kept on hanging round our place.

When, in the end, I says to Father I was sick tripping over her, he just tells me to let her be. Well I was flummoxed! I couldn't understand this change of tune. For wasn't it he himself says to me only six months before that he was sick of Mary under his feet? Seeing as I didn't know what was going on, then, you can hardly blame me for losing my temper in the end. The time come, as I knew it would, when Mary drove me as far as I could go. She just wouldn't give over about Father and her in "the old days" as she called them, though her voice was a lot politer than mine. (Some of England had rubbed off on her.) No matter how many times I let her know I wasn't interested, she still kept on and on. Of a sudden, I let fly. But it didn't fizz on Mary. Lord no! She just sat there like a saint while I was shaking from head to toe. It was then she dropped the thunderbolt. As cool as you like, she says she had cancer. In other words, she was dying, though by the look on her face it didn't bother her none. You can imagine how all this made me feel. Guilty's not the word. And she didn't help things any by starting to apologise. But I wasn't going to let her get the better of me in that way. By God, no!

"Dying doesn't give you no right to put in on other people," says I to her. And I told her I knew a dozen at least in the parish was as near death's door as she was. And they weren't spending their last days sitting in Father's house. Call me heartless if you like. But if I had my life to live over, I'd say the very same thing again. Sick and dying people took up most of Father's attention. And I didn't think it was fair.

To give the devil his dues, Mary took it well. And she didn't bother me no more after that. Though she continued to call to see Father.

I kept a close eye on Father in the weeks after to see how he was taking the news. Either he was a very good actor or he wasn't put about at all. In the end, when curiosity got the better of me, I broached the subject with him.

"Sure isn't she going to God?" was all he says. It was then, for the first time, I felt any real pity for the girl. I wondered she kept coming to see him at all if all she was getting was that kind of old chat out of him. Of course, I can only speak for myself. But I know it used to drive me mad the way Father took death in his stride. And Mary's death was no different than nobody else's whenever it come. He says the Funeral Mass the same way he'd say any other. Not a flicker of feeling showed in his face as far as I could see. But there's more to life than meets the eye, as they say, and what I'm going to tell you now, I never told another soul before.

The wake was held in Father Bosco's house, for Mary's man had left her six months before. I went over to give Marie Coll a hand with the catering, for you know yourself what wakes is like. Between handing out drink and keeping an eye on the spongers who did a round of every wake in the parish just to fill their stomachs, Marie and me had our hands full. Not but nothing went unknown to me, busy and all as I was, in them three days. That's one advantage in being a priest's maid. Nobody expects you to open your mouth, so you can keep your eyes and ears open instead. People come in droves from all over the town on Father Bosco's account. I mean no disrespect to the dead, God forbid, but Mary was that stuck-up, she didn't have a friend of her own about the place. Either Father Mann or Father Bosco himself was there the whole time to lead the praying. The last night come and only the family was left about the coffin. Still they kept on saying the Rosary to keep themselves awake and stop themselves from thinking. It was about midnight when I joined them. Then, for the first time, I noticed neither of the Fathers was present. I presumed they'd been called away and put no pass on it till I went up to the bathroom a half hour after. This was when I heard them at it, hammer and tongs, in Father Bosco's room. They were arguing in loud, angry whispers, about Mary, and shoving one another about the place. Father Mann sounded the loudest.

"I had no choice," says he.

"How convenient for you!" says Father Bosco back at him.

"What was that supposed to mean?" says Father.

Father Bosco's voice was shaking. "Mary loved you, and you turned your back on her."

"You don't know what I went through," Father says, getting all high and mighty. "You don't know what it is to love somebody and have to give them up."

"How would you know?" says Father Bosco. It needed no mindreader to know he was bitter about something else besides his sister.

I couldn't believe my ears. Two priests fighting like that, like two cats. The louder they got the more scared I got somebody was going to come up the stairs and hear them at it. So I tip-toed to the bathroom and banged the door as loud as I could; loud enough for them to hear and catch themselves on, I hoped. Father Mann was first out of the room. His face was blazing and his collar was all ruffled. Not but he looked me straight in the eye and headed down the stairs. He acted cool as a cucumber, like nothing had happened. Then Father Bosco appeared and made a bee-line for the bathroom. I could see he'd taken the worst of the wear which didn't surprise me none, for he was aye the nervous sort. A bit like a woman if you come right down to it.

Praying was done for me for that night, though I went back

downstairs again. All I could think about was them three—Mary, God rest her soul, and the two of them upstairs—and what had brought them to this sad state of affairs. I couldn't make head nor tail of it. But this much was clear to me; something went far wrong somewhere for so much misery to come out. It didn't pass my notice neither in the days after the funeral that, contrary to what I thought in the beginning, Mary's death had a powerful effect on Father. Dying didn't get her out of our road as I hoped it would. (I don't mean to sound cruel or speak ill of the dead, but you've got to understand she was making Father's life a misery.) Instead, her being dead give her an even greater hold over him. He started talking about her. And whereas in the past he was aye criticising her, he had only good things to say about her now. He aye spoke about her in the same breath as his mother. I could imagine the pair of them grinning at me from the other side of the grave. God forgive me but I envied them getting his affection like that, for nothing. While I attended him hand and foot all day. And for what? I have to say though, I felt sorry for him in the end for he couldn't bring himself to love a living person. I figured the only reason he could love Mary now was she was out of harm's way and he could make her anything he wanted her to be.

Looking back, I seem to have spent most of my life jealous of one person or another when it come to Father. I resented the people that come to him with their problems, when me that lived under the same roof didn't dare open my mouth to him unless it was something to do with the housekeeping I had to say. There was one lot of people he had more time for than anybody else in the parish, though, and that was the youngsters. This earned him a good word from everybody that knew him at the same time as it put me off youngsters for life. For they were aye getting the attention I wanted. Now I'm not proud of these feelings. I'm only trying to be honest with you. Maybe if I'd got more attention myself as a youngster, I wouldn't have begrudged it to other youngsters in turn.

It's my experience that when you live with somebody you're often the last person they think about. I've heard many a woman complain the same way about her own man. That's one reason why they come to Father—to get the notice they didn't get at home. But what I aye wondered was where the men went when they were wanting the same attention, for I never seen them hanging about the convent, wanting to speak to the nuns.

Not but Father and me did have the odd time to ourselves and I never forgot one of them. I mind one evening in particular way back in the late Fifties. I'd been working for Father no more than a year at the time and there was a power strike. The men at Coolkeeragh was wanting more money. And this evening I'm talking about, I'd just set Father's dinner down in front of him when the lights went out. It was the long nights into the bargain, and every house between ours and the river was left in the pitch dark. Father didn't seem to mind, though, for he'd been hearing Confession in the dark most of the evening anyway. But I had my work to do. I groped my way to the pantry where I knew I could lay hands on a store of candles I'd put by for such an emergency. The place looked like the chapel on Christmas night when I was finished with it, and the candle-light made Father's big eyes shine. I was noticing this when he laid down his knife and fork on the table. He'd barely touched a bite which wasn't like him in the evening. "I couldn't see where my mouth was," says he and laughed a nervous sort of laugh at me. Very little put him out of his way of going. I was going about my business with my own candle in my hand when he asked me to stay. "You may as well," says he, "for neither of us is able to do anything without the power." Father never drank heavy but he drank a bottle of wine that night and told me all about himself and Bishop Cleary. I could see clear as day it was a real sore point with him. It was a battle of wills, says he, and Bishop Cleary wanted to keep him in his place. He says, as well, that he didn't like the way the Bishop treated me neither. Which was right and decent of him, bearing in mind he wasn't obliged to notice anything on my account. That was a grand evening, I mind. Most of the time, though, him and me just stayed out of one another's road. His duties kept him out of the house anyway, and out from under my feet.

Money was another sore point between him and me which we never did manage to thresh out on account I was too scared to bring the subject up. And it never occurred to Father there was anything wrong with our arrangement. His family had money, you see. Not a terrible lot but what seemed a terrible lot to me. (All I had to go by was anything I owned myself which amounted to nothing since the House took the few savings my ma and da owned. Michael, Dympna and me never seen a penny of it. So anybody had anything seemed rich to us.) Father Mann wanted for nothing. From his socks to a swanky car, his family bought him everything while, at the same time, I was working without proper wages. And any money Father himself had was laid by to line his nephew's pockets in later years. I can't help thinking some of that money should've come my way, if only in the shape of regular wages. Not but every priest's maid suffered the same in them days. I had to go to Father for everything I wanted.

Plenty wives I knew was in the same predicament. Our Dympna, for one. Though her Charlie was good to her the same as Father was good to me, he kept his hands on the purse strings. And she couldn't buy herself a stitch without getting his permission first. Still and all, she had one thing I didn't have—a family of her own to look after. And I'd tell her this any time she complained to me. But she'd only tell me I should appreciate having my life to myself. I was jealous of her and she was jealous of me. That's about the sum of it. Father used to say if all of us looked hard enough we'd aye find somebody worse off and somebody better off than ourselves and we should appreciate what we'd got instead of wanting to swap with somebody else. But I never seen it that way. If you want my opinion, that's just an argument well-off people use to keep the not-so-well-off as themselves in their place. And I never listened to it.

The very house I lived in wasn't my own and never would be my own if I lived there a hundred years. It belonged to the Church and would always belong to the Church. And the things was in it belonged to Father and would go to Father's family when he was finished with them, even though it was me cleaned and polished them every day. It used to drive me mad the way Damon—that was Father's nephew—checked every-thing was in its proper place whenever he come into the house, as if I was going to run off with anything.

Time wasn't standing still neither. And, though I was only twenty-four at this time, I was beginning to feel old already. Old would be all right, I says to myself, if only I had something to show for it. But I hadn't. And it's wild feeling the years slipping by and having nothing to show for them except a mess of wrinkles and grey hairs. It was the Sixties into the bargain and everybody was breaking free. Then the Sixties never reached the Presbytery. Or not till the Nineties anyway.

It was about this time Marie Coll and me fell out. She had

aye called in ours on a Saturday night (and done other houses the rest of the week.) But her and me was never that great, the reason being Marie was cast in a different mould and easy pleased. She was aye out at hops and socials with people at the same time as she never put much pass on them. Not like me. Her Father Bosco was just a mouth to feed and nothing more as far as she was concerned. If he didn't pay her any heed, then she didn't notice or she didn't care. Marie could be content in herself and I had to admire her for that, except I sometimes thought there was little to her in the end. But maybe that's just spite talking. One thing I know for sure. The only reason she kept in with me was for fear of missing a bar. And I didn't have it in me to tell her where to go, though many's a time I had a good mind to. Anyway, she come into ours this day, looking all high and mighty. I knew by the set of her, there was something eating her. She was spoiling for a fight, I knew, for she plonked herself down in front of the kitchen range so as to be right in my road. I says nothing, though, and let her pick at the sandwich I give her. Just as I was putting the dinner out, she started asking me all these old questions about the stew I was making. And when I says to her I didn't have time to answer her, she huffed. Says she, I never had no time to talk to her any more, not since Father become the parish priest. So this was it! She was jealous of me on Father's account. I should've known as much because, for months before, she'd been boasting how her own wee priest was sure to get the job, and how she'd be moving with him to his new house. Course I never put no pass on any of this talk at the time. I knew right well my own Father Mann would get the job, for wee Father Bosco, God love him, didn't have the clout. As well as that, I knew something else Marie didn't know. Father Bosco wasn't at himself and was likely to fall off his feet any day. The Bishop would never give a man like that the job of parish priest. Marie took it awful hard. But I don't think that give her the right to let it all out on me. "You won't be wanting to talk to the likes of me any more," says she and throws the crust of the sandwich down on the floor. That put the hat on it.

"Keep y'r hair on," I says to her. Sure enough, I could've told her how Father was sending me to cookery classes now on account of the big nobs was visiting him. And I could've told her about all the extra jobs I had to do. But I didn't have a mind to. I was glad to see the back of her. Not but I missed the company the rare time, and the crack. I was aye sure to know the latest so long as Marie was around. None of the other priests' maids in the parish would ever come near me. Old Annie Zachery never laid foot outside the Bishop's house. Even if she did, can you imagine her and me having a heart to heart? And Father Green's maid, Martha, was a dour, empty-headed kind of a girl—the sort that collected knitting patterns from the *Woman's Own*. I have to say, I did try talking to her a couple of times in the chapel yard. But she hadn't a word to say to me. I heard of tight-lipped but that one took the biscuit. Still, I seen her and Marie Coll rattling on ninety to the dozen the Sunday after Marie and me had rowed. Well, Marie was welcome to her and she was welcome to Marie as far as I was concerned.

CHAPTER FOUR

Christmases was rough without a family, I have to admit that. Though I can't ever mind a good one even when Michael and Dympna was around. Not but we weren't a proper family which was likely the reason. And Christmas at Bethel House left a lot to be desired in any case. It was that time of the year things was always happening to me. Father, in his wisdom, used to maintain an anniversary acted like a poultice on the mind and brung a lot of stuff out. And maybe there was something to his story, for my birthday was about that time, the eighth of December in fact. And my mother's anniversary was on the fourteenth. As a child, I was aye ailing at Christmas time. One year I even broke my leg falling off a wall. What I was doing up there in the first place, I can't imagine for, like I says to you before, I was never one for danger. I also tried my first drink and my first cigarette at Christmas, though I took to neither. The same year, I fell out with Michael over Ruth who was his girl-friend at the time. I left Thornhead and I come to be Father's maid at Christmas.

Christmas of sixty-nine was another year I mind for that was the year my aunt Grace (or Gráinne, as she liked to call herself) come back from America. And I heard the story about my ma and da. And why Michael, Dympna and me had been put in Bethel House in the first place.

I was setting up the crib in the living room at the time. Not that I was one for cribs myself but Father liked them. I never could stand the soppy look on Mary's face and the way Joseph was weighed down under an over-sized halo. And the crib we had was a queer jumble of pieces. Mary was two times the size of Joseph and the infant had come in plastic from Woolworths. Then there was the shepherds. I don't know where they come from, but they were a shifty assortment if ever I seen the like. I had to be careful the way I laid them all out too, for Father was wild particular. The first year, after I got them wrong, he knelt down on the ground and showed me the exact way they ought to be. There he was, him on one side of the crib and me on the other, like Joseph and Mary themselves. And he read me a line from the Bible explaining why the infant should always go between the ass and the ox. "Lord," says he, "Thou shalt manifest Thyself between two beasts." That year Grace come, I mind I was having terrible trouble with the infant. The wee cutty who had given me a hand to put him away the year before had wrapped him in the tinsel come off the Christmas pudding. The tinsel had stuck and bits of cake and raisin was lodged in his armpits and ears. Not to mention the fact he reeked of brandy and needed a good wash. I was washing him in the kitchen sink, and taking the colour out of one of his eyes as I mind rightly, when the doorbell rung.

Seeing as it was the day before Christmas, I figured it was one of the men come to leave in a load of coal or timber or a bag of spuds for the dinner, and I still had the infant in my hand when I went to the door. It wasn't any of the men, though, but Dympna. And she had a strange woman with her. Dympna never says "hello," just barged in as cocky as you like. "This here is our aunt Grace," says she. And from the grin on her face I could see she was all pleased with herself. I can still mind the piercing blue eye of the infant staring out at me from the heart of the dishcloth at the very same minute. "She's come over from America to see us," Dympna says.

The woman was made up that bright, I could see for myself she wasn't local. She had on these chequered bell-bottoms, a red choker and a black hipster belt. And her hair, which was dyed strawberry blonde, was set up high on top of her head. Her nails was painted too, the same colour as the choker.

I kept my distance from her even she says she was my aunt. Grace, on the other hand, acted like she knew me. She was all over me, calling me "sugar" and "honey," though I knew for certain she'd never set eyes on me before in her life. She was downright pushy, if you ask me.

Dympna was looking round for sign of Father in the meantime.

"He's gone down to the Bogside," says I, for them was the days of the civil rights marches, if you mind. And there was aye wee skirmishes there every day. Like the other priests roundabout, Father did what he could to keep the peace.

"Good," says Dympna and plonks herself down in front of the fire. She had a wild heavy way of throwing her backside in the seat that give me the shudders. It never seemed to occur to her I lived in the house as well as Father and looked after the furniture. She threw a present at me across the table. Bedroom slippers, it was, the same thing she give me every year. Grace had something for me too. "Well? Aren't you going to open it, honey?" she says.

I have to confess, I was spoiled rotten with presents at that time. Good people in the parish was aye giving me things on account I was Father's maid. The only problem was, I never got anything I liked which put me off presents all the-gether. The idea of asking for something particular never occurred to me. I'm not saying I wasn't thankful, God forbid. But people had fixed notions what a priest's maid should want. At one time, I mind, I had six pairs of Rosary beads, four sets of thermal underwear, six hot water bottles, kitchen knives without count, three cookery books and three prayer-books put by me. And, all the time, women was calling at the house with baking Father and me had no call for. Most of it went to the dog.

I took a look inside the red bag Grace had given me. God preserve us all! I never seen nothing like it, except on the TV. The choker was purple, and the pencil skirt was purple and yellow check. They were both the in thing—all figure hugging and sexy. Clothes like that was only fit for a movie star as far as I was concerned. And I couldn't ever see myself wearing them, not in a month of Sundays. Says I to myself, Grace must've been expecting somebody else and here she was, faced with me in my tweed skirt and aran pullover. I felt dead embarrassed.

But Dympna was as bad as me when it come to her appearance. The youngsters had put the years on her (as they will on many a woman) and she was terrible fat. Not but she couldn't blame the weans alone for putting the beef on. She ate a lot of rubbish. I couldn't mind the last time her face seen a powder puff neither. This was depression, I reckoned. For Charlie, her husband, kept her tight under his thumb.

"Why don't you try them on?" says Grace to me and she pointed a red fingernail at the bag in my hand.

My biggest fear was Father would come in in the middle of it and I wasn't sure what he'd think. Still and all, I did as Grace says for fear of hurting her feelings.

The clothes made me feel that awkward, I was afraid to come out of the bedroom when I was done. In the end, Dympna started roaring on me. Patience was never a strong point with that one.

"All you need now is a touch of make-up," Grace says when I finally worked up the nerve to show my face. And she wouldn't give over till I let her put some of her own powder and lipstick on me. I can tell you now, them five minutes felt like eternity. I was aye used to making the tea when people come in, you see. That way I didn't have to entertain them or say nothing that drew attention to me.

While Grace was doing me up, I noticed Dympna had opened the slippers she brought me. She was ripping the labels and pulling the fluff off them as if they still belonged to her. It needed no mindreader to see she was in a bad temper. Maybe Grace was paying me too much notice for her liking, or she hadn't got as nice a present and was jealous. Then she was always that touchy; it took little at the best of times to make her mad at me. You see, I was a sharp reminder of the past on account I'd spent my entire life in Bethel House. And Dympna wanted to forget that above anything else in her life. I suppose it's only fair to say as well, she was expecting her fifth at the time I'm talking about. And she was aye crabby when she was expecting. What with not being able to get around in comfort and the prospect of all them extra nappies to clean, I suppose I'd no call blaming her. She'd just moved to Craigavon into the bargain. Charlie had followed the work after Monarch Electric shut down. And Dympna hated it there. She says it was a soulless place. So, between one thing and another, she was like a hawk that day.

Now Grace's going to America in the first place had aye been a sore subject with Dympna, Michael and me. For, according to the story anyway, she could've stayed and looked after us when our mother died. Instead of which she gallivanted off to America, leaving us to the nuns in Bethel House. I was wondering whether she was going to stay this time or if she was just here to ease her conscience—on a guilt trip, so to speak. But I didn't dare ask her for fear of rubbing her up the wrong way. I was out of the way of asking questions anyway. The people that come to Father's door usually had their story ready in their mouth and needed no encouragement from me. So I kept my mouth shut and let Grace tell me what she liked and leave out what she didn't like.

She'd come back to see us "children," she says. Children, I says to myself. She's still living in the past. And sure enough, that's where her mind was heading. But it wasn't on our account. Lord, no. I seen already she had no interest in us beyond a passing curiosity that was satisfied the first minute she stepped foot inside the door.

"I've been in America now twenty-seven years," she says. "Your mother always said I didn't fit in here and she was right."

From this talk, I took it she still believed she done the right thing when she left us behind. And I seen no more pity in her eye for our poor mother when she mentioned her name.

"I shrink to think what would have happened to me if I'd stayed here any longer," she says, and she screwed up her eyes like she'd just tasted something rotten. "I was only a month in America when all that old Catholic stuff dropped away from me. No harm to you, Brigid," she adds, as a kind of afterthought and looks at me all innocent-like.

God knows, maybe she didn't mean me no harm like she says for I seen no sign of spite in the way she looked at me. Still, I never give her a smile nor nothing.

Dympna, on the other hand, couldn't barely cover a look of

glee when she seen the effect Grace was having on me. Not but I kept a straight face. I wasn't going to give her the satisfaction. It worried me, though; she might've been talking to Grace about me behind my back, saying how religious I was and all that. I could be sure she wouldn't say nothing nice about Father neither.

Grace took a hold of my chin. "Look at the colour of you!" says she. "You look like you've never seen the sun in years. And those clothes you were wearing when I came in! They're like something your grandmother would've worn. You might as well be in mourning. How can you stand it, locked up here, year in, year out?"

"I'm not locked up!" says I, biting the head off her. Least I didn't feel I was locked up. Or not till she says to me anyway. But I wasn't going to let on a thing like that to her, nor Dympna neither. Knowing my sister, she'd only jump at the excuse for laying into Father. She might even say something to his face when he come in. And I couldn't risk the chance of that.

Grace left me not knowing who or where I was. It would be a lie for me to say I wasn't pleased to see her. She made my life with Father seem distant for a while, and give me a different slant on things. I could even imagine myself waltzing out into the world, happy as Larry, like everybody else, and leaving Father behind. At the same time, I didn't like her talk about religion "dropping away" from her like it was dead skin she had to get rid of. I couldn't get my mind round a life without religion. So, in the end, I come to the conclusion I'd never be nothing but a Cinders, like in the story. Grace was no fairy godmother.

Then she says, bold as you like, "Have you ever had a man?"

Well, I didn't know where to look, I was that embarrassed.

"Never worry, honey," says she, taking pity on me. "Even with my experience I can't tell if it's worth it or not. Men are always telling you what to do. Take your father for instance."

This mention of my da brought me down to earth with a plonk. And I seen right away he was the reason Grace had come. From the scrunched up look on her face, I knew she was testing out the water as to how Dympna and me felt about the man. Dympna bolted off her seat at the very mention of his name and my own jaw dropped. I remember that much. Then the two of us just stood there, not able to do nor say nothing and waited for Grace to say whatever it was she come to say.

"Your father asked me to talk to you," says she after a minute had passed and we were over the initial shock. "He wants to see his children."

"What about Michael?" Dympna piped up. As ever, she was on the look-out for people making differences between us. And she hardly seemed to heed what Grace was saying in the process.

"I've already spoken to Michael," says Grace, "and he won't have anything to do with it."

Well! I ask you. Could you blame him? After my da doing the damage he done?

Father Mann was aye saying Christmas was a time for the family. But this was taking it too far, if you ask me. What did Grace take Dympna and me for? Saints—like wee Marie Goretti? That man who called himself our da killed our ma and none of us was going to forget that in a hurry. Not one of us had breathed his name in over ten years. And I didn't see the point in ripping open old wounds now. The past is the past.

It took no great skill on Grace's part to read our minds. Her next strategy was to tell us the whole story. Of course we'd

and blood and it was easier for her. She didn't go all the way round, though. She waved for us to follow. I just stood there, nearly too scared to breathe. As for Dympna, poor soul, she hadn't been looking at herself since she come in the place. And I knew, from the desperate look on her face, she was dying to leave. She kept fidgeting with a paper-bag of apples she'd brung to give to him. He shifted, sudden. It happened that quick I had to hold Dympna for fear of her running away. Not but he went real still again, like a statue in the chapel, and just sat there staring up at us with this long, white face. His lips was chapped and, by the glazed look in his eyes, I seen he was doped out of his mind. I felt nothing.

Like she was the first one to move, Grace was the first one to open her mouth, too. She couldn't abide silence, whatever was wrong with her, and started into this old rigmarole. It hardly seemed to matter what she was saying, just as long as she was droning on. She started off by asking my da how the nurses was treating him—as if he'd just come in to have his appendix out. And she laughed real loud about the man in the ward who took hold of Dympna. Half way through telling the story though, she seen it was no laughing matter and let the ending drop. Then she started going on about America but that had no effect on him neither. All this time Dympna and me was standing well back out of the road. "Let's go," Dympna mouthed to me and give me a sharp tug. I'll tell you this about our Dympna; she never was a good one for standing her ground. I mind one time when we were youngsters, she run a mile and left me standing, just to get away from a black man. (Black men was rare in Derry in them days.) And this time was just the same. Grace dried up as soon as she seen she was getting nowhere. All of us was about to go, when my da made a reach for Dympna. He made a quick grab for her by the hand. God love poor Dympna, she jumped that hard, she spilled the apples all over the floor. She couldn't thole him touching her, I knew, from the terrible look was on her face.

"Anne," says my da, taking her for my ma.

Grace leapt at this chance to butt in and started to explain to him who we all were. My da was all through-other, I seen, as he tried to take in what she was saying. It took him a good quarter of an hour to get the bare facts straight. And who could blame him with Grace ranting on at the rate she was going and stumbling all over herself. Poor man. I figured it must've been a rare clear moment he asked to see us in the first place. He'd been buried away that long in this hell-hole called a hospital, and pumped that full of God-knows-what to keep him quiet, he couldn't hardly mind his own past. He picked up one of the apples that had fallen and handed it to Dympna. His hands was grimy and there was dirt under his fingernails. He must've been working in the garden, I thought to myself.

"How many grandchildren have I?" he says to Dympna as soon as Grace had piped down.

Dympna says to him, though there was a terrible tremor in her voice.

"And you?" he turns to me. "How many have you?"

Of course I told him I didn't have any on account I was Father's maid.

"Father?" says he, "why I'm your father, girl."

So I explained who Father was.

"No daughter o' mine is slave to any man," says he and banged his fist down hard on the arm of the chair.

Grace got on her high horse at this. "It's a pity you didn't think that way when you were married to my sister," she says.

"You talk too much, woman," my da hissed back at her under his breath. I seen he was raging mad from the way he gripped his head in his hands. But he was too scared to raise his voice for fear of being heard. "Priests," he turns on me again. "Priests is no different from the rest of us. I hate them—priests! It was one of them put me in here. He says to me he was doing me a good turn. Me! I'd as rather've taken my chances in a court of law any day."

There was no mistaking the clergy was a sore subject with my da, the same way they were with Tim. But one good thing come out of it, at least. I seen Dympna's eyes light up for the first time from she come in the room. And Grace appeared to be enjoying herself no less, listening to him ranting and raving the way he was. And he wasn't finished yet.

"What did he, a priest, know about a crime of passion?" he says. "Setting himself above me like that, and pushing me around when I hadn't the strength to help myself. Priests, I loathe them. The ones that come in here! They come again and again wanting to hear my Confession. Just 'cos I married one of their own kind, they think they've a right to my very soul. But I'll never give in to them. Never! So long as I live. I've got the better of them. My soul's my own and I'll damn it to hell if I want to. It's you women give them these notions about themselves. Bowing and scraping the way you do. But let me tell you. They're just like the rest of us, under that cassock. They're just like the rest of us. They're just like the rest of us," he kept on saying to himself.

I swear, I'd never heard nothing like it in my life before, not even from Tim and he loathed priests more than anybody else I knew ever did. I was desperate to get out of the room, as you can imagine. But my da rose out of his seat and got in my road. And he was fly about it, too, for he checked first to see if he was being watched before he moved a hair. "Them nuns and priests conspired to keep you away from me," he says. "They haven't the spunk to have youngsters of their own, so instead they bully other people's around. They leave them unfit to be whole human beings—like you, daughter," he says to me. "But you're as bad. You let them do it to you. You chose a civilised kind of battering. For that's all it is. Battering! Like I did to your mother. I suppose you think you're too good to go the road most women do."

Funny, Tim and Dympna had says the same kind of thing to me before. But I never felt that rotten about letting anybody down as my da made me feel that day. Mas and das can be wild tormentors.

The Sister was outside the door by the time he had finished this tirade and she seen him laying down the law inside. She barged straight in, the way she did before, and ordered us out with her finger pointed at the door.

"That's it, Lizzy," my da laughed at her. "That's a woman for you!"

As you can imagine, it was terrible difficult to set my mind to anything that evening. My thoughts was going round and round, over the story Grace had told us and over the terrible things my da had says to me. When I looked in the mirror, I seen his face staring back at me. My face was just like his and this scared the living daylights out of me. My eyes was even glazed from crying that much. I was due to go to Confession that night as well. But I couldn't bring myself to go, certainly not to Father. No way could I bring myself to say to him the things my own father says to me. I was scared to hurt him in the first place. And I was scared what he might think of me. So I went to Father Clerkin instead. He was hearing in the Cathedral at ten. When it come to telling my sins, I couldn't put nothing in words and kept stammering and stumbling over myself. Father Clerkin got more and more annoyed. "What do you want to tell me, daughter?" he kept saying. As much as I could clearly say was I felt guilty for my da being in that place. I don't think Father Clerkin would have noticed if I says I committed murder. For, as soon as he had the sin out of me, he give me three Our Fathers and told me to go in peace. Three Our Fathers didn't seem enough to me but I knew better than to quarrel with him. I says the prayers like he says. But, as I turned to leave the Cathedral, another guilt took a hold of me. I never seemed free of some sin or other in them days. Now I was feeling I'd betrayed Father by going to Father Clerkin instead of him. For, before that night, I never kept nothing from him.

After Confession, I went to Midnight Mass for it was Christmas Eve like I told you. Men straggled into the chapel from the pubs just before midnight. The chapel was cosy. The darkness in the place, before the procession come in with the light, was a relief to my sore eyes. I was so tired after the day, I could've gone to sleep kneeling there. But I gripped my candle hard and concentrated on that to keep me awake. On the stroke of midnight, the procession carrying the light come in through the back doors. I aye liked that second or two when I could see the faint glimmer of light from behind and everything in the chapel was cast in giant shadows. Then all the altar boys spread out along the aisles and lit the congregation's candles from their own. Father had given out the Sunday before that nobody was allowed to cheat, but I seen a man using a lighter a few seats away from me.

Old Mrs Boyle, who was on my right, held out her candle for

me to light. She was the oddest old woman; wore clothes you'd never see nobody else wearing, not even in them days. I'd only ever seen the like in films and then they were on women a good deal younger than her. She'd sat in that same seat as long as I could remember. (I'm sure if she was living to this day, she'd still be sitting there. And she'd look just the same, the way she always looked.) But as I lit her candle that night I seen old Mrs Boyle in a way I'd never seen her before. She was of an age with my father, I thought to myself. When she was young my father was young, though judging by the look of her now, it was hard to believe she'd ever been anything but old. For she was that ugly. Her face was covered in black wrinkles and she had long hairs growing out of her chin. I think I stared at her too long that night for she dropped candle wax on to my hand and give me a dirty look.

The electric light come on and Father told us to blow out our candles. A gorgeous smell of burning wax filled the chapel. It was then I heard a hard thud coming from the front row. A woman had fainted—the same one as made a habit of fainting at the smell of candle wax. It aye fell the lot of whatever poor man was sitting nearest her at the time to carry her out. Everybody stared at him as he picked her up, the way King Kong picked up Fay Wray in the film, and carried her into the sacristy. I used to wonder what it felt to be picked up like that.

The wax old Mrs Boyle had dropped on my hand was hardening. I noticed some other drops she'd spilled during the ceremony was congealing on the seat in front of her. That night, I mind, I lost myself in the familiar sounds of the Mass for they made me forget the day like something in a dream. I mind, in particular, looking up at Father as he says the Offertory. His arms was stretched out the way the priest was supposed to do at that part of the Mass and his hands looked that clean. Not like my own father's, I thought to myself. And I admired Father for the way he was. I chipped the hardened wax from the back of my own hand.

Father waited a few minutes at the foot of the altar after the Mass was over. Behind him the congregation was singing the "Adeste Fideles." The force of feeling in the music that night swept me away with it. Old songs, old hymns 'specially, aye affect me that way. Like the sea, they make everything else in life seem small and unimportant. Then the procession left the altar and made its way back to the sacristy. There was a hushed rush for the back door and a growing surge of excitement. Children's voices rose above the rest. Christmas had really begun.

That night I spent threshing round in my bed. I dreamt I was getting letters through the post from people I hadn't thought about in years. Father and I was travelling about in foreign parts in the dream. He tried to way-lay the letters but I got the better of him.

It was still pitch dark outside when I rose to go to the dawn Mass. I aye liked the dawn Mass best or maybe I just liked the dawn, for everything seemed possible at that time. The day seemed endless. Father talked about this feeling that very morning but he spoke as though it was a certainty. "The dawn," he says, "which the Church calls on us to greet this morning is the dawn of a day which shall see no end." Of course that day ended like every other day. I think it was Tim McFaul told me once that Christmas used to be a pagan festival when people celebrated the sun. And the ceremony was held at dawn, or so people believed, for no written accounts of the celebration was ever kept. It's rare to think that people believed trees and animals—or in this case the sun—had spirits and souls. Though I could almost understand it that morning. The sunlight was that cold and bright it stung my eyes.

Only a few stragglers ever attended the dawn Mass. It was mostly women who come out early so they could make the dinner when they went home. God! How I envied some of them women come into the chapel in front of me. There they'd be, fifteen minutes before the Mass started sometimes, with their heads in their hands and praying away to the Tabernacle. I never had the same faith them women had. I wished sometimes I could leave my life in God's hands the way they did. A few men with spaniel looks and caps in their hands hung about the back-seats. They looked brow-beaten. As I passed them on my way in that morning, I smelt the drink off their breath. Some of them hadn't been to bed, was my guess. I was sure one of them hadn't been for I'd seen him, a half hour earlier, from the Presbytery window, loitering about the chapel door. And I knew him for one whose wife locked him out regularly. There was never any style at this Mass. That was another thing I liked about it. You could turn up in slippers and nobody would say a word.

The lights was low in the chapel and the place was so still you could hear a pin drop. Father could barely make out the responses, the congregation was that small. With their being so few, people was afraid to open their mouths for fear of being heard. "Quietness may be desirable in women," Father says, "but this is neither the time or the place." This minded me on something the Bishop says the first day ever I went to help out at his house. But I put no more pass on it at the time and smiled like all the others. When it come the time for the sermon, Father says he'd leave it out for the women had enough to do without listening to him. God love him. He aye had a thought for the poor women that had to go home and cook the dinner. Come Communion time I was the first to rise. It wasn't like eleven Mass when there was a rush for the altar rail. Somebody had to make the first move and it was usually me. Of course I'd been to Communion the night before. But, with it being Christmas, we could go to Communion as many times as we liked. As father stood over me that morning I smelt the altar wine off his breath. It minded me of the men at the back of the chapel. I noticed none of them had come up for Communion. All of the women went, though. And, as soon as they were back in their seats I noticed they all bowed their heads in their hands to pray. Now this was something I never felt comfortable doing myself on account I found it difficult to pray. I'd try to fix my mind on God right enough, but it had a habit of going its own way. And I'd find myself thinking about something else, like the meat for the dinner I'd forgotten to take out of the freezer, or the episode of *Peyton Place* was on the television the night before.

I went to the later masses that day as well. (Since I come to work for Father, I hadn't missed a single Mass he says.) It was a different breed of people attended eleven. They were what you might call professional chapel-goers, not the troubled, religious kind you got at other times. They usually dressed for the occasion and come in families. You were likely to see more hats than headscarfs and more patent than leather at that Mass. New cars, new dresses, new husbands got their first airing at eleven Mass. Come the Offertory, half crowns, not sixpences was thrown into the basket. Sometimes a father could be seen handing round silver to his youngsters so they could put it in the basket themselves. Father Mann aye give the crowd its money's worth. He give them what they come for at eleven which was a good sermon. And, after the Mass was over, he'd join them for a yarn in the chapel yard. It was then you spotted the little priests and nuns to be. They were that well-mannered. Some families just seem to breed that kind of youngster. Other boys and girls met at this Mass; some even courted when they thought nobody was looking. But Father was the only man I ever had eyes for in the chapel. When I watched him, standing up there on the altar, I felt as proud as punch. He was the same man I'd given breakfast to, but not the same man, if you know what I mean.

One of the privileges I had as a priest's maid was that I could slip away from Mass through the sacristy door. Only the sacristan and me had that honour. And most days I took advantage of this for I wasn't fond of company. The Christmas day I'm talking about was one of these days. After Mass was over, I slipped out the back way, though the sacristan was mad I walked over her newly bleached floor. I was passing the toilets at the bottom of the steps when I noticed a young couple hanging about outside the gents. They were kissing and cuddling. But as soon as they seen me, they pulled apart like they had got an electric shock. I could hear them sniggering and giggling after I walked away. Maybe it's just being alone makes you feel old before your time, but I felt terrible old that day seeing that pair. And I felt terrible young at the same time. Only shame and the fear they would see me stopped me taking another look at them. I had no intention of leaving Father, of course. But I couldn't help wondering, once in a while, when my life felt terrible empty, what would've happened to me if I hadn't been Father's maid.

Father's brother, Ronan, and his family come to see him that

Christmas, the same as every Christmas. Ronan was educated. He had a way with words that scared the living daylights out of me. But that aside, I could take him or leave him. His wife, on the other hand—Miriam her name was—had her knife in me from the start. She was a bad one, that, if you know what I mean, for she was aye out to stir things up between Father and me. The kind she was, she disapproved of any woman living under the same roof as a priest, 'specially if that priest happened to be Father Patrick Mann. I don't know what she took me for. That day she decided to introduce Father to the idea of the "new priest," as she called him, that is a priest who done rightly on his own without a maid. There was already one of the breed I knew of in the Long Tower parish.

"It's not good having a stranger in the house," Miriam says to Father. She was aye trying to get rid of me. But Father never paid her any heed, though he kept her going, just for the fun of it.

"Brigid's no stranger," Father says to her. "Far from it!"

Miriam would find excuses to get me out of the room, then complain about me behind my back. But, as it happens, I heard every word she says from the kitchen.

"That one's deep," she says. "There's something the matter with her. She trembles. She acts like a frightened rabbit."

Well, Father only laughed at this, and Ronan with him. This made Miriam madder, as you can imagine.

"Don't you ever worry," she went on to Father in the same posh voice she aye used to him, "don't you ever worry some of her father might come out in that girl?"

"Are you suggesting she's likely to kill me in my sleep?" Father says, real slow, pretending to take her seriously.

Angry or not, I had to laugh at the idea myself.

"Of course not!" Miriam snaps back at him. She couldn't stand it when he didn't take her serious. "You know what I mean. I think that girl has bad feelings in her."

"If she has, I've never seen any of them," Father says. He was real serious this time.

"You give that girl too much freedom," Miriam says. "You never correct a thing she does." God but she was full of spite, the reason being Father liked me better than her. And I aye had the notion she liked Father far more than she ever liked Ronan. At the same time, I don't think she ever forgive him for preferring God before her. As for me, I don't think she understood a woman who took it on herself to be a priest's maid. She was that selfish herself, she didn't know what it was to want to help somebody else. Miriam was the worldly type, you see. You only had to look at her dripping jewellery to see that. And the clothes she wore. She dressed as fitted a headmaster's wife in Derry in them days. But it wasn't on Father's account alone Miriam was jealous of me. She envied me as well because I had my life to myself. As far as she was concerned anyway, I was free of the messy entanglements that come with being a wife. And we all knew Miriam's marriage to Ronan wasn't good.

To be fair though, Miriam wasn't the only one to blame. What she got away with, she got away with only because Father let her away with it. And he let her away with plenty so long as she kept him amused. If you ask me, he should've put her in her place in the beginning and stamped out the vicious streak in her. Ronan was as bad, for he used this situation with me to get back at Miriam. He'd keep her going just by joking to Father how nice it was to have a maid instead of a wife. And he'd do this to her face. I mind one thing in particular he says. "You know where Brigid's been," whatever that was supposed to mean. "And sure isn't she cheap and trouble-free?" says he that day when Miriam was doing me down.

Damon—the son, that is—rarely opened his mouth in our house. He seemed more interested in Father's silver collection that day. Indeed, he looked to me to be making a mental list of it when I come in with the tea. He was an accountant, you see. "A priest of the new faith," I heard somebody call him one time. And he looked after the family's finances which included Father's. This day, he noticed a chalice missing from the cabinet. Father turned to me to explain where the chalice had disappeared to. At the same time, I could feel the others' accusing eyes boring into me. I didn't need no imagination to know what they were thinking.

"You give it to Father Bosco," I says to Father, then grinned at them. "Father Bosco's own was stolen from the sacristy, mind, and you give him the lend of yours."

"Sure enough," says Father back. Though I don't think he minded at all, or cared less what had become of it for that matter. "What would I do without you, Brigid?" he says.

Course, I didn't answer this. Damon wasn't going to trust me anyway so what was the point in saying anything at all?

"Better remember to get it back," Damon says. "That chalice is worth a bob or two."

CHAPTER FIVE

Maybe it was a penance on us both—what happened to Father Mann. "To humble our pride and remind us of the sentence of death." Father was telling us off the altar just the Sunday before how we should "welcome Lent" and "welcome suffering." Suffering might be hard currency in Heaven, but I never could bring myself to value it here. That kind of thinking's sick, if you ask me. And I defy anyone to tell me what good ever come of the terrible suffering that started that Ash Wednesday in nineteen-eighty.

I mind the morning well. I was baking bread in the kitchen when Father come in. Now, it was rare for Father ever to step foot inside the kitchen door. And I seen from the tormented look on his face, something was wrong. And he was in a daze like a spell was cast over him.

"Jessie," he says to me.

I waited for him to go on.

"Jessie," he says a second time, and it was only then I discovered he was talking to me. Of course, my name isn't Jessie, as you know; but Jessie was his mother's name. He'd mixed us up, I thought to myself, and put no more pass on it at the time. He was looking for nothing much in the end, just an old *Ireland's Own* he'd set down somewhere and forgot about. God love him, he aye liked the *Ireland's Own* for the riddles.

It wasn't hard for me to find the paper. I knew right well

where he'd left it—in the lavatory where he had a bad habit of taking it. And, after that, I give him his breakfast. With it being Ash Wednesday, I made sure to give him the same thing I give him every fast day: black tea, porridge and dry toast. (Honest to God! I spent half my time putting taste into food and the other half taking taste out of it to keep him happy.) He was aye terrible particular about the fast as long as I had known him. You can imagine my surprise then, when he demanded a decent breakfast that day. But I didn't argue with him. Apart from anything else, I was glad on my own account, for when he wasn't eating he expected me to starve as well. I give him what I knew he liked and come out of the house in a hurry. Mass wasn't for another hour still. But I couldn't stand being in the house with him in the mood he was in, whatever was wrong with him.

It was a crisp, clear February day I mind, and, Lent or no Lent, I was in a mood to please myself; 'specially after the way he threw the breakfast back in my face. I'm not saying I was unhappy working for Father. I wasn't. It was a good job being a priest's maid. Still and all there was some days, like that day, when I just wanted out of it. There's many a wife or husband feels the same on a bad day, I would bet my life on it. The only problem was, I didn't know how to please myself. That's something you learn like everything else. And I felt guilty into the bargain, for the nuns had brung me up believing it was wrong to please myself. On the other hand, I see now, I was that used to misery, I didn't want to let it go. It was what I knew.

Now it fell my lot to open the chapel in the morning; this also meant unlocking the door to Father's sacristy. Any other day I would've turned the key in the lock and gone away but this day, whatever got into me, I took it into my head to go in and have a look around. I hadn't ever been inside this room before, though I'd been working to Father for over twenty years at the time. The reason was I found the place terrible forbidding—more forbidding than his bedroom even, where I went in to make his bed every day. All he ever kept here had to do with the chapel. I think that was why it struck the fear of God into me. None of it had anything to do with me. The kind Father was, he kept everything to do with religion to himself. He never let me near his soul, if you like. It would have taken a very special woman to get that close to him. And, with the exception of his dead mother, I don't think he ever knew any special women in his life. I hadn't any business in the room that day, as I says, but I went in all the same. My main fear was finding something I shouldn't. Don't ask me what I meant by that, for I can't say. I opened the wardrobe door. Inside was the beautiful vestments he wore at the different masses. Father Green had ordered him a set just like his own. Violet, green, red, black and white, they were, and all embroidered with Irish patterns. (The Americans is wild ones for things like that.) I'd never touched them before. God, but they felt gorgeous. I run my fingers all over them, the way you would over silky underwear. I felt that guilty. What would Father say if he ever knew?

The altar bells which was rung at every Mass was sitting on a table in the corner of the room. The tiniest touch of a finger made them tinkle. And sitting beside them was the urn of incense Father used for Benediction during Lent. I sniffed the incense. God, I was addicted to that stuff. I think I can say with some safety, I understand glue-sniffers. There was a chalice on the table as well, heaped with communion hosts. They were unblessed, I guessed. Otherwise Father wouldn't have left them there like that. So I helped myself to a handful. Before I swallowed them, though, I remembered my fast and spit them out again. There was no place to put the chewed up mess so I wrapped it in a hanky and hid it in my pocket. On another table in the middle of the room was the ashes for the next Mass. Father would use these to anoint the congregation. "The Church during the season of Lent, preaches the death in us of the man of sin." The words welled up out of nowhere at me. Notions like this was drummed into me that hard, I don't think I'll ever forget them as long as I live. I dipped my finger in the ashes, the way you'd dip your finger in a pot of jam if you were hungry, and put my finger to my brow. It was when I was looking at myself in the mirror, admiring the big black dab, I heard footsteps coming up the nave of the chapel. I wiped off the ashes with the hanky I'd used to hide the hosts and managed to be back out in the corridor when the sacristan come along. I kept my head down for fear the guilt showed in my face. (I never was a good liar.) Not that the sacristan paid me any heed. It never occurred to her that I'd do anything wrong anyway. I looked that harmless.

During the Mass, I found it awful hard keeping my place on account of the guilt was preying on me. It was only when the sacristan nudged me in the ribs, I noticed something was wrong.

"He's forgotten the Epistle," says she in a loud whisper, right in my ear. "Maybe some of us should go up and tell him."

Course, I knew she meant me to go up and do it. So I stepped up to the altar rail and had a word with Father. He was grateful for the reminder, not angry like I was scared he might be, and went back to saying the Epistle. I mind the reading well.

"In those days Ezekias was sick even to death, and Isaias the son of Amos the prophet came unto him, and said to him, 'Thus saith the Lord; take order with thy house, for thou shalt die and shall not live.' "

My face was beetroot red for shame by the time I got back to my seat. I wasn't used to making a spectacle of myself like that, even though I was Father's maid. But it was either that or have an argument with the sacristan. And I knew from the dogged kind she was, she wouldn't give an inch to save a life. Then, I was the soft sod let her away with it.

The rest of the Mass went all right as far as I could gather. Father minded everything he was supposed to say. And afterwards, he blessed the ashes and give them out. Mainly women, as was usual, queued up to get anointed; the men was that backward. I stayed back till the last for I liked to see the others filing past. It made me that proud of Father to see the way them women looked up to him as he thumbed the Sign of the Cross, in ashes, on their brows. I felt they were looking up to me as well. At the same time, I have to confess now, another feeling come over me. I was jealous. I was jealous because Father treated all us women the same. And I wanted more from him. I wanted him to treat me special. When it come my turn to be anointed, I was still that angry I pulled away. And Father noticed, though he didn't put much pass on me. I needed every ounce of will power I had in me, to hold my head in place the second time. My brow tightened with the ashes. May God forgive me, but I would've rubbed them off there and then except I was scared of being seen.

In the chapel yard afterwards, the tongue-wagging was all about Father; how he'd stumbled through the opening Antiphon and forgotten the Epistle. "There's a man with something on his mind," says one who was aye setting himself up as an authority on people. "If you ask me, that man's not

124

well," another says back. It made me anxious to hear them talking about Father like that. Him being a priest and all. It didn't seem right.

Nor did Father do nothing to ease my mind neither. Instead of doing his round of the sick, which is what he usually done on a Wednesday, he went straight back to the house that day—without saying a word to nobody neither—and locked himself in his study.

Lizzy Bone, a wee woman that wasn't that well off, had come in for his butts in the meantime. (The poor woman couldn't afford her own cigarettes, so I saved her Father's ends.) And, to keep her amused, I was showing her Father's picture in *The Journal*. The yearly outing for the old age pensioners had been the week before and Father had gone along to keep them company. God help them, the old people used to be that proud of him going with them, they'd talk about it the rest of the year. The whole crowd of them was pictured outside the Strand Hotel in Buncrana where they'd gone in for their dinner. It was while Lizzy was going through the faces, passing insulting remarks on every one the way she did, that Father come out and says he wanted a word with me. Now this sounded serious. The first thought crossed my mind of course was he'd discovered I was in his room and was calling me in to give me a touch. So I just sat there on my side of the table waiting for what was coming. But he didn't open his mouth for ages. All sorts of things went through my head, like something had happened to Dympna or Michael maybe, and he was too scared to break the news to me (for I'd heard a banshee two nights before.) Or he'd decided he didn't need a maid no more. He was aye joking about going off to the missions and leaving me. It wasn't like him to beat about the bush when he had something to say. So this day he scared the living daylights out of me. He just sat there, fidgeting with a book—*The Lives of the Saints* I think it was—and turning the ends of the pages all up. Never before had I seen him this flustered. He was usually that even tempered a man, and always in charge of himself.

"Brigid," he says, eventually. (Not but he kept his eyes on the cover of the book.) "Brigid," he says a second time, "I think you ought to know I'm not well."

"Then go to the doctor," I says, not taking in the seriousness of what he says. I was that relieved he'd opened his mouth at all.

"I've been to the doctor," he says. "He tells me I've got Alzheimer's disease."

Well, as you may know, this left me no further forward. But Father seen my quandary and explained himself so as I could understand what he says.

"In two years' time," he says, "I won't be able to read one of these books." And he took a dreadful look round the room. (Father had a grand library, though most of the books was in foreign writing and made no sense to me.) I took it then, he was going blind.

"No, not blind," he says. "But, believe me, before two years are up, I won't be able read a word of these. I'm losing my mind."

This was too much for me to take in. I never heard the like before in my life.

"This morning," he says, "I tried for two whole hours to remember a poem I knew by heart. *God's Grandeur* it was called. I managed to remember the title but nothing more of it. And every day I wake, Brigid, I'll have forgotten something else. One day I'll wake up and I won't remember your name. Could you bear that, Brigid?"

126

What was I to say? I couldn't look at him, let alone answer such a question. It just couldn't be true what he was telling me. He was the picture of health. But, when I says this to him, it only got him all riled up.

"I'm losing my mind, Brigid. I'm losing my mind," he roars, real desperately, at me. I never heard feeling nor fear like that in his voice before. "Priests," he says, "rant happily about death and the joys of Heaven when it's someone else's life they're talking about. But it's another story when they're talking about their own."

I couldn't stand to hear him talking that way. And more; I was afraid old Lizzy would hear him from the kitchen. For if she got wind of it, the whole story would be round the parish in no time. So I tried my best to calm the poor soul down by giving him a pleading look. But it was no use. He was that wound up there was no stopping him. And all I could do was hear him out.

"I could deal with bodily death," he says. "I had prepared for death in the normal sense but not for something like this. I'm slowly becoming an idiot, Brigid. Much consolation it is I'll be too far gone to care when the worst comes. I wish I was a saint but I'm not a saint. How could I be with the anger's in me now?"

"Even Our Saviour lost his temper once in a while," says I to him, feeding him the line he fed us off the altar many's a time. Not that it did him any good. It seemed anything I says to him just made him far worse in the end. Poor soul. He felt alone for the first time in his life. After what had happened to him, he was convinced God had deserted him—if He was ever there in the first place. And he wanted me to make up for what he was missing all of a sudden. Then he got vexed when he seen I wasn't up to it and pretended he didn't want no more to do with me. "You needn't stay," he turns on me with a crabbed voice.

"The Bishop assures me I'll get the best of care."

"Nobody says nothing about leaving," I says to him. I was for staying and I says as much to him. But Father was a proud man. "You're free to go," he says to me time and time again. "You're free to go. You're free to go." This kind of talk didn't bother me none. What did bother me though was the way he railed against God himself. Tim, I would have understood. Or Father Jack if he had a drink or two in him. But not my own Father Mann. I never heard him raving at God that way before. And it pulled the carpet right out from under me. "I've been cheated," he cried out of him like a man who had just been swindled out of his life-savings. "I've been cheated. Inside a year I won't be able to function as a priest. It makes me wonder if I did the right thing being a priest at all in the first place. Do you think I did the right thing, Brigid?" he turns to me.

Well, how was I to know? It wasn't for me to answer a question like that even I was able. Still I says, "Of course." What else could I say under the circumstances? Not that it mattered what I says for he wasn't paying me any heed anyway. His mind was too busy trying to figure out a sensible reason why this terrible sickness was visited on him of all people.

"I turned my back on life. Now life is turning its back on me," he says.

This kind of old talk wasn't the kind of thing I was used hearing out of him. And I says to him he was too hard on himself. But he wasn't finished yet.

"I scoffed at common sense. Now sense is deserting me," he says. One after another he kept coming out with all these fancy reasons why things had turned out the way they done for him. I can't mind the half of them, for to tell you the truth, they didn't make sense to me. Father was aye talking over my head. What I do know is, soured and angry as he sounded, he seemed to be getting some comfort out of blaming himself and I left him to it. Things was easier for him to bear if he could make some sense out of them. Whereas I never seen no sense in nothing anyway. And I was way past believing there was justice in the world. The world was never a scary place for Father, poor soul, till that day; the day he discovered nothing made sense and he wasn't in charge any more.

"I'm likely to end up jabbering nonsense, Brigid," he says to me. "Do you understand that?" And he rammed his face right up to mine, like he was already starting to act the idiot. Jesus, Mary and Joseph, but he scared the wits out of me that day before I was able to get used to him.

I tried my best to tell him God was testing him. "As you y'rsell preached to us off the altar many's a time," I says to him, "Our Saviour's suffering give meaning to his life." But I might as well have talked to a brick wall.

"I can't helping thinking..." he says, his mind wandering way off on its own. "I can't help thinking I might've married and had a few children by now. I might even have married you, Brigid," he says.

Well, that done it for me. I seen then, clear as day, Father wasn't himself any more. He never used to talk to me like that before. And it made me terrible uncomfortable. It was only when I was outside the door, I felt excited at what he says. I'm saying this now. But I wouldn't have admitted it at the time, not even to myself. The guilt of it would've been too much to thole.

My first thought, once the truth had sunk in, was how this sickness of Father's was going to affect me. Don't get me wrong! My heart went out to him. But I didn't want my life to change. All my working life I'd been a priest's maid and I didn't want to be anything else. I'd relied on Father always being there. He'd been my mainstay, my reason for living, for over twenty years. And I couldn't imagine living without him. Worse than that; I couldn't bear the thought of being on my own.

The disease galloped at first, though Father fought it tooth and nail. In the first six months, I seen little change in him. If anything, he had more energy. He fought off tiredness with sheer obstinacy alone. Some nights he'd sleep no more than three hours, and when he rose, he'd go at everything like a mad bull. He'd sit up till all hours reading when there was nothing else to do. Whole days and nights he'd spend with people he hadn't seen in years. I suppose it hurt me when he didn't spend more time with me. Then, why should he? I was only the maid. It also seemed to me he was trying to prove, so long as he had it in him to do so, that he could cope on his own without me. It can't have been easy knowing the condition lay ahead of him. Few of us would go back to being infants, I'm sure, for that's the condition he was looking forward to. I mind well the first time I ever had to remind him of an appointment he forgot to keep. He ate the face off me and told me he minded the appointment himself. Or the first night I helped him to his bed after he'd fallen sound asleep at the dinner table. He'd made a day of it, poor soul, when he didn't have the energy. Out at a wedding first, then putting up the new Stations in the chapel, and, after that, he'd been entertaining the Bishop with dinner. When it come pudding time, I seen he was falling asleep in his chair. Once, he started awake and called out, "Jessie." Bishop Cleary was that embarrassed, he made a quick getaway and left me to put Father to bed. While I was doing this, Father started going over all this old stuff. He wasn't raving, exactly, for there was plenty sense in what he says. He talked about the time his mother kneeled over him and prayed to God on his behalf that he'd be a good boy.

"My father used to scold her," says he, "for he maintained she made too much of me. I loved flying a kite in them days," he says. "We'd catch wasps in jam-pots full of water. I loved to go fishing in the Faughan with my father." God love him, he was grasping at every memory he could lay his hand on. This was his last, desperate bid to keep hold of himself. He had the look on him of a drowning man. "My uncle Pat's wedding and my auntie Fanny's funeral. And all the time I wanted to be a priest. I remember. I remember." God help him, he had so much to remember—so much to forget, as well. Not like me.

I was embarrassed at hearing all this talk out of him but I couldn't rightly shut my ears. (You can't shut your ears as easy as your eyes and mouth.) It didn't seem right to be listening to things as private as that.

Not but everything wasn't gloomy. Father could be light-hearted into the bargain in them days; the way he used to be at the very beginning before the Bishop got the better of him. We'd play cards in the evening. And sometimes he'd tell me stories about Maynooth. He told me about the big bell they called Vox Dei (the Voice of God that means in proper English) that woke them up every morning and called them to chapel and meals. They weren't allowed to smoke, he says, though he himself smoked forty a day until he got ill. And they had to smuggle novels into their rooms, the priests was that scared books would make sinners out of them. Their rooms was searched regular, he says. And they weren't allowed to visit one another at night. All this made Bethel House sound like a holiday camp.

Maybe it's wrong of me to say such a thing under the circumstances, but them days I spent with Father was the happiest days of my life. Though I still had to deal with Miriam interfering. I mind, in particular, the night she come on us playing chequers in the drawing room. Not knowing Father was ill at the time, she got the wrong end of the stick and let the brunt of her anger out on me. Coward that she was, she didn't dare take me on in front of Father. She cornered me in the kitchen instead. "You ought to know your place," she says to me. "Father has better things to do than to waste his time on you." Imagine! The cheek of her! And me looking after him the way I was.

The sickness Father had was a terrible sickness. I might have packed my bags in the beginning if I'd known how terrible it was going to be. May God forgive me, but many's a time I wished Father was dead instead. Anything but that Alzheimer's. He was living and breathing at the same time as he wasn't Father any more. It was a living death. (Not but he got Extreme Unction from the Bishop the day after he found out.) And I couldn't feel nothing any more. I didn't dare for fear I might up and leave him and I couldn't live with myself after that. So life was terrible for both of us. At the same time as I'm saying this, the real truth of the matter is that most things was just the same. For all I had to do was attend to Father's basic needs now as then. It was the sickness brought home to me how rare my living with Father had been. If such a devastating thing didn't make no real difference, then there can't have been much worth talking about between us in the first place.

The worst part for him was the beginning when he knew what was happening but couldn't stop it. I told him he was suffering like Our Lord suffered in the garden of Gethsemane. But this only made him worse. The sheer terror showed in his face. He minded me on a gunman I seen on the run one time.

132

Only the terror on his face was ten times worse. God but it's terrible to see a man scared, 'specially one you come to rely on the way I come to rely on Father. Anger at God was the only thing kept him going in the beginning. Then, when he was tired raging, he'd pray for a miracle cure. I don't know which was the worst, seeing him that angry or that bowed under. The disease got him in terrible scrapes into the bargain. Without meaning to, he'd fall out with people—people, that is, who didn't know he was sick and took offence at something he said or did. He'd forget people's names and forget to keep appointments. Sometimes he'd mind the appointment right enough, but turn up in the wrong place. He'd get tired. His speech slowed down. And he'd lose track of a conversation very easy. Naturally enough this got people riled and did nothing for Father's good name in the parish. It was pride, I think, made him keep his sickness from the people for as long as he did. He made it a point that nobody at all should find out the truth until they very definitely had to. All this time the sickness ate into him and he never breathed a word about it to a living soul, not even to me after that first day we talked about it. From a man had been so out-going and full of himself, he turned into a backward, bitter person. And he seemed to loathe himself more than anything else. It was hard for me to thole, just looking at him when I could do nothing to ease his pain. Not but my own pain was just as terrible. The agony was that great sometimes, I wanted to go far away and never come back. And when the truth did come out, as eventually it had to do, everybody seen Father's suffering. Nobody seen mine.

Miriam it was let the cat out of the bag. She told a friend of hers. From there, the news spread like wildfire round the town. Up till then, though, not another soul, except me, seen Father

133

at his worst. And I kept my tongue in my teeth, for I was scared even then in case the Bishop or Father's family would take him away from me.

As soon as the word was out, of course, Bishop Cleary ordered Father to gave up his parish duties. This nearly broke Father's heart as you can imagine. The Bishop says to me as well he didn't want me working to Father any more. And Ronan and Miriam says the same. Their plan was to get a trained nurse for him which would've been more respectable, I suppose. But Father, God love him, stood up to the lot of them. He'd hired me, he says, and he'd fire me if anybody was going to. Miriam was even more jealous than she'd ever been when she heard this. It got under her skin when she seen that Father was dependent on me, for she was that possessive of him. She would've stopped at nothing to get rid of me. She tried to talk me into going in the beginning, and, when that didn't work, she seen doctors and tried to have me proved unfit. She even got another priest to ask me to come and work for him. But none of her tactics worked. You can be sure, I was careful of her after that. One slip, and she'd have me out on the street in no time. That woman's mind never stopped going. If you ask me, it was a terrible waste of mental energy. I could see she was thinking all kinds of things—like I was going to turn Father against her (as if she needed any help to do that.) She couldn't stand to think that, in the poor state he was in, Father would open himself up to me. I think that maddened her most of all. That, and the physical side of things which come later. But I fed on Miriam's hate the way I fed on Magdalene Cook's hate many years before.

The next stage of the disease was the worst for me; for that's when all the upset come. God help us all, but it was bitter to see Father lose power of himself like that. Him that was such a lively, good-looking man. And, I'll tell you now, I did think Father was good-looking though I never admitted as much to myself as long as he was well. It made me mad as hell to see that terrible sickness making an idiot out of him. Nor was this the whole of it. I got mad at myself as well for I couldn't quell this powerful feeling of disgust that was growing in me. Honest to God, he'd talk that hard, like a youngster, he'd slaver over himself, and he'd wet the bed at night. It's hard seeing a man going to bits in front of your eyes like that. Me, I like a man to be in charge of himself. And Father was in charge of himself till that damned sickness got a hold of him. I'm sure he had urges, like any other man, but he was aye master of them.

If it had been another person it happened to—myself, for example—the effects would have seemed far less agonising. People like me, you see, that've been put down all their life know what it's like to be overcome and know how to cope with it. But Father had been up in the world. He had that much further to fall. And there was the tragedy of it.

The first time he threw a tantrum on me, he fired some scrambled eggs across the kitchen. Sure, I knew it was the sickness made him do it, but I cried my eyes out for hours after. He was that selfish, I says to myself. Not but I was just as bad when I come to think of it. I couldn't hardly believe the words was coming out of my mouth that morning. "You spoilt thing! You ought to be ashamed of y'rsell! All this noise and mess for nothing!" And all the time he was whingeing and whining like a wean. He whinged that hard in the end, he started the very dog barking. God in heaven help us, but it took all the strength and patience I had in me to stay with him after that day. Of course, it broke my heart to see him suffering. But it wasn't his life alone was wrecked. Mine was in bits as well. Everything I'd ever come to rely on was taken away from me. Even God. I wasn't sure that He existed any more. The terror was that terrible sometimes, and my mind went that blank, I'd sit for hours in the one place doing or thinking nothing at all. And I'd come out of it no more sensible and no more rested. The awful thing was, you see, I had a choice in the matter and Father didn't. I could've upped and left him any time. Only guilt and fear stopped me. But before long, I begun to rely on the Bishop, the way I used to rely on Father, to make decisions for me. Father wasn't going to die, or not for a long time anyway. So I accepted his sickness in the end. It was just the price I had to pay for keeping my place.

The human spirit's sturdy. There's little a body can't adapt to given the need is strong enough. And that's what happened to me. After the disappointment sunk in, I come to enjoy the way Father needed me for it made me feel far more important than I ever did when he was at himself. I even got myself into such a way of thinking, it didn't matter to me he ate flowers and bits of coal. He was still Father and the man I looked up to. Only, at night, sometimes I'd wake up in a cold sweat and wonder what in God's name I was doing with him. The man's an idiot, I'd say to myself. He can't even dress himself. But come the morning I'd be calm again. Better the devil you know, I'd say to myself.

It was the Bishop's idea to move us to the country. If you ask me, he sent Father away like the lepers was sent away in the Bible. He wouldn't have put it that way, of course. But the fewer people seen Father in his condition, the better, as far as Bishop Cleary was concerned. Father had become a bad advertisement, if not a downright embarrassment, to the clergy. He couldn't control his mouth or his bowels. And he made passes at strangers, men and women alike. Not but the Bishop provided well for him. It was aye his boast, after all, that the Catholic Church looked after its own. (Pity he didn't extend this to include me in later years.) I think another reason he sent Father away was for fear of the notion some people had about mental illness. You see, there was them in the parish, and some that should've known better, that thought Father had some badness in him; though they wouldn't have said as much to his face. God forgive them. But people like that is awful backward in their thinking. Superstitious, is what they are. I had it in mind—as a dig—to ask the Bishop if Father shouldn't be moved to Strove Bann or Glannagalt, in Kerry, for there's supposed to be a cure in the water there. I never had time for such boloney myself; the same way I've no time for Knock and Lourdes nowadays.

All my life I'd spent in Derry. So I needn't hardly tell you it was a terrible wrench leaving the place. Columcille can't have felt more sorry than I did, though I wasn't going nearly as far away. At the same time, I didn't dare open my mouth to complain. Not that it would've done any good anyway, for I had no real say what happened to me so long as I was working for Father. Don't get me wrong. I'm not complaining. Before this there'd aye been somebody telling me what to do and I'd gotten used to it. It's not as if I wanted to make my own decisions. As I seen it, the world was divided into two sets of people: them that give the orders and them that took them. The first lot was made up of the nuns and priests and teachers. Then there was the rest of us. And I wasn't wanting to change that.

The worst part of all was leaving the few people I knew and the places I liked to go around Bishop Street. (I hadn't been out of sight of Bethel House all my life.) On the other hand, it was a relief to be away from the Troubles for the Catholics and

137

Protestants was at one another's throats in them days. And I'd be kept awake with the raids, and the sounds of women banging bin-lids in the wee small hours of the morning.

Death is what it felt like, leaving Derry. That's the only way I can put it. And I'm not exaggerating neither, for I hadn't a notion where we were going or how people was going to take to us. Everything depended on Father. And I was afraid, with him not being a proper priest any more, nobody would pay us any heed. And where would I be then? What I hadn't figured on, though, was his sickness would give him a whole lot more importance in some people's eyes. As one woman put it, he was "nearer to the angels." Now this was a nice turn-about. If only all our fears was answered the same way.

Bishop Cleary had more money than sense, judging by the house he picked for Father and me. It was a gazebo of a place, set in a big clump of trees, about three miles from Dungiven. And there wasn't a living soul in sight for miles. I mind as well the day we moved. Midsummer's eve, it was, and there hadn't been a drop of rain all week. It was that hot, indeed, the tar was boiling on the road, I mind. Father Jack had been shifted to Dungiven a couple of years before as it happened. So it fell his lot to taxi us. Father Mann took the seat up in front beside him, and left me the back seat to myself. Though I did nothing but roll around and bang my head on the roof. Father Jack was that drunk he took the bends awful hard. Honest to God, my heart was in my mouth and my stomach was churning. All the time I was saying Hail Marys in the back, Father was laughing his head off in the front. God help him, he thought he was in the bumper cars. (I mind him telling me once, he loved the amusements as a wean.) Not but I had to laugh myself in the end, Father Jack was that grand a turn. (He always was when he had a drink in him.) And he was full that day as usual. He made fun of poor Father O'Dowd who was that set in his ways Father Jack says the PP after his name stood for Petrified Priest. "I'm afraid I'll have to say no," Father Jack mocked him. Father O'Dowd was aye saying that. You couldn't help but laugh at Father Jack, he had that good a knack of doing voices, and there was aye something to his story. Once we passed Altnagelvin hospital, I hadn't a clue where we were going. Not but Father Jack was ready with a running commentary. Everything he says I took with a pinch of salt, for I knew fine well he was enjoying my ignorance. And I never put it past him to take a hand out of me.

The fields of rape-seed was like a picture. And the cattle looked that peaceful just chewing their cud. But the smell in some parts was enough to turn your stomach. Silage, Father Jack says it was. It smelt rotten and I was praying to God we wouldn't have to live with it where we were going.

In Dungiven itself, every second house we come upon was a pub. And old-fashioned they looked, too—dark and dingy and in need of a lick of paint. Father Jack must've felt at home here, I says to myself. The couple of shops there was looked awful paltry and I wondered if Father and me would ever have enough. Outside the Orange-hall, a big crowd had gathered to practise for the Twelfth. God! There was no getting away from it. We were out the other end of the town before you could say Jack Robinson. Fifteen miles to Derry the sign-post says, though, in my mind, we felt an awful lot further away; an awful lot further from home. I was feeling homesick for the very first time in my life. I know it may sound rare, but I felt hemmed in by the open fields and the mountains on either side of us. After spending my whole life in the town the country didn't agree with me.

Father Jack stopped a hundred yards from the gate; the idea being, we could get a decent look at the place if we walked in. My legs was stiff when I stepped out of the car and my stomach was sick, for Father Jack had taken the last mile or two at an awful speed. All along the sides of road, the hedges was filled with hawthorn and honeysuckle, and there was a beautiful smell. But the midges was pestering Father something terrible. "Swat the buggers," Father Jack kept saying to him. The road we were on dwindled into a narrow lane and still I seen no sign of the house. Father Jack pointed his finger at a wee swirl of dust twenty yards in front of us. "That's the sí gaoithe—the wind fairies," he says, "travelling from one home to another." I didn't pay him any heed for Father Jack was aye trying to fob off old yarns on me. He thought I was that gullible. And he was forever launching into gaelic when no one that spoke the language was about to correct him. He was nothing but a show-off, if you ask me, and liked to play on poor people that hadn't the same education as himself. You could bet your life on it, he wouldn't utter a word of gaelic or mention the fairies round Bishop Cleary. He knew too well what was good for him. Anyway, I wasn't going to give him the satisfaction of taking any notice that day. His head was big enough already without me adding to it.

Father Mann kept his arm hooked in mine. And I was watching his step at the same time as I was looking out for the house. As things happened, I couldn't've missed the place, it turned out to be that big. My first thought was Father and me would rattle round in it like two peas. All this for a dying priest, I says to myself. And it made me wonder what the Bishop had in mind. I got angry as well, the more I thought about it. To think of all the ordinary men and women who had to settle for a bed in a ward in the Nazareth House. (The Nazareth House was the place in Derry where old people went when they'd nobody willing or able to look after them.)

We'd just come round the corner of the gate when a man, carrying a scythe, sprung out on us. It was Tim McFaul, no less. He was older and fatter about the stomach, but in the face, in the eyes in particular, he was still the same Tim. And he give me the shock of my life, though I seen from the dour look on his face I didn't surprise him none. He must've known I was coming. Without as much as a word to me, he held his hand out to Father Mann. Father Jack, in his big, brash way, never noticed nothing and made the introductions. "Tim, here, will be doing the garden for you," he says. "He does a fine job on the chapel grounds."

"I've been seeing to the roses," Tim says, apologising for the clay under his fingernails. "They're past their prime, I'm sorry to say. But there's always next year."

I could see he was too scared to look at me. And all the old liking I used to feel for him come back again. It did my heart that much good to see him, I could've cried my eyes out.

The Bishop had sent us to the back of beyond. That much was already clear to me. While the whole of us was walking down the lane to the house, Father Jack says to me how himself and another chaplain did all the work was needed. For, though the parish was big, ten odd miles from one end to the other, the number of people was very small. And they weren't demanding neither, he says. Not like the people in Derry that were aye banging on your door. They had some thought for a man's privacy, he says. And Father and me wouldn't be bothered none.

On the other hand, I says to him, Bishop Cleary demanded

the people was to be asked to Mass in the house. Father could still say Mass, you see. Though I looked on this as a miracle at the time, I know now the only reason he minded the Mass when he minded nothing else was because the stuff was drummed into him that hard. Even Alzheimer's couldn't beat the Mass out of him.

The Bishop had seen to it that Father's things was brought ahead and laid out as near as possible to the way they were in Derry. All them things Father had no call for any more! All them books! But they belonged to him. And where he went, they went; and I'd look after them. The Bishop maintained at the time he kept up this appearance of normality for Father's sake. But, if you ask me, he only done it for the people that come into the house. The picture of Father as he was before the sickness, was kept in front of everybody's mind. I don't think it crossed the Bishop's mind the pain I felt having to live with them reminders day in, day out.

My own stuff was heaped in a rough pile in the smallest bedroom in the place. Big and all as the house was, I'd been given the servant's room nevertheless. Not that I minded really, for I never was one for big rooms; not since the dorm in Bethel House. I hadn't many things needed storing anyway. Living with Father meant I needed very little. I had my own bed, a single bed. (Father aye had a double one.) Apart from that, the only things I owned was my clothes, a couple of holy relics from Lourdes and a store of *Woman's Own*. I kept my room, like I kept my life, bare and spare for I never could stand clutter. And there was aye enough to look after with Father's things.

Seeing as Father Jack was there with us, and able to keep an eye on Father, I took the opportunity to have a quick squint round the place. It was hundreds of years old, with fancy

142

ceilings and grand wooden fireplaces. There was a musty smell about, right enough, but I put that down to the place being empty so long. The kitchen, which was my main concern, was big and filled with heavy wooden presses. It had a Rayburn cooker, just the thing for the job; and a wide, wooden table. I looked forward to baking bread on that. There was plenty outhouses as well but they weren't my concern. I kept myself confined to the inside. From the windows in the attic you could see as far as Feeny on one side and Limavady on the other. It was here I used to come in later years when I needed to get away from Father. I fell in love with the house—Knockmaroon, it was called—for it reeked of the past. I used to imagine the people that lived there before me and I'd see them coming and going around the place, in old clothes, like they still lived there. I sucked the excitement out of the walls of that place the way you'd suck the flavour out of honeysuckle. I drew life out of them, the way I used to draw life from the stories Father told me when he'd come in from a day's rounds in the parish. That was in the time he was well, of course. The way he was now, he couldn't make a proper sentence, let alone tell stories any more.

He asked me that day when we were going home to Derry. Though I tried to break it easy to him we were never going back, he just wouldn't listen and kept asking me the same question over and over again. It made my heart sore listening to him. The night was even worse, for then he got scared the way a wean would get scared if it didn't know where it was and seen the darkness coming on. And he wouldn't go to his bed for me neither. Every time I tried to rise him off the settee, he got cranky and threw a tantrum on me. There was nothing for it in the end but use brute force to get him on his feet. It was all I could do to make him put one foot past another. Between conning and coaxing, I got him as far as the bedroom eventually. I left him there, sitting on the side of the bed, with strict orders to put his pyjamas on. But when I looked in a half hour later, he was still sitting in the same place with a miserable pout on his face and he hadn't removed a stitch. That was the first time I had to undress him and put him to bed. I was that scared, though, I waited a whole hour before I could work up the courage to go through with it. And while I was doing it, I kept praying no one would come in on top of me. My eyes I kept fixed on the statue of the Virgin which Father had aye kept at the foot of his bed. Other nights after that, I'd fix my attention on anything happened to be handy in the room: the light bulb, a certain ring on the curtain rail or some pattern in the wallpaper. There's many a thing a body does because they have to. And putting Father to bed was one of them things for me. Not but I didn't think about it when I was doing it. I didn't dare. Though there was many things I mind about it now; things that affected me at the time but I never allowed myself to dwell on. I mind the terrible sense I had the first time I seen him without his collar. I know it's silly—the notions you can take into your head. But I never thought of Father without a collar. It just never occurred to me he took it off, not even at night. I took his shirt off first and his vest after. Father had a young body. It would've been easier for me, I think, if the sickness had showed on him. But it never did. My mind was in a terrible quandary. One minute I'd be feeling disgusted with him. The next, he'd turn on me with them lovely big, blue eyes. And it was all I could do to stop myself putting my arms round him. He looked that innocent.

I sat many's a night with him that first summer we spent at Knockmaroon. Poor soul! In the state he was in he was too scared to fall asleep, and he wouldn't be content unless I stayed with him. The nights was that quiet (not like the nights in the town), I fell asleep myself in the chair many's a time and didn't know till I come to in the morning. Only the rare time you'd hear the howling of a dog or the croak of a raven. There was never a wind about the place; only a light breeze blowing through the trees. (The person that owned the place before must've reverenced trees right enough, for the place was surrounded by them.) And the sky was that clear you could see every star there was in Heaven. After a while, when things settled down, Father usually dropped off about twelve, and I got some time to myself for the first time all day. Though all I was fit to do most of the time was sleep. Father wore me out that much.

I think the shift to the country robbed Father of the little sense he had left in him. For he took a turn for the worse about this time. Everything had to be done for him now, from feeding to cleaning. I didn't dare let him shave himself for fear he might cut his throat. And then what would people think? Mealtimes was a real nightmare. He'd keep getting up while I was trying to put food into him and wander off to another room. I don't think he even knew what hunger was any more. Then other times I'd come on him gorging himself in the kitchen. (Things like turpentine and weed-killer wasn't safe round him.) He'd eat or drink anything, and spill what he didn't take over himself. Days when he was contrary, he wouldn't let me wash him neither. He'd scream his head off if I come within a mile of him with a cloth. So I had to let him be some of the time. There was nothing else for it. And he'd stink to the high heavens. He put no pass on it himself. Only me had to put up with it. But taking him to the toilet was the biggest handling ever I had. He wouldn't stay still there neither. It was like training a youngster, only worse. But I managed that well, that neither the Bishop, nor no one else, seen much change in him. Not but I got terrible tired in the middle of it all. My biggest fear was falling asleep on him. I even locked the doors during the day for fear of him wandering off on me. He'd got this habit, you see, of roaming about the house in the middle of the night. Some nights I'd come on him sitting staring at the air in some strange corner. He'd have no notion where he was or what he was doing there, or even care. Night and day meant nothing to him any more. As time went by it was harder to keep him in his bed. I tried tiring him out in the middle of the day, the way you'd do with a wean, in the hope he'd sleep better at night. But it did no good. Whatever the nature of the sickness he had, it enabled him to get by with little or no sleep at the same time as it wore me out looking after him.

Our lives, Father's and mine, was confined to the four walls of Knockmaroon except the odd day, his birthday or something, I'd take him out for a change. He liked that. We'd go to a cafe. The place was a grocery shop really, with a tea shop tucked away behind. But the main thing was nobody put any pass on us there. We'd order tea and Paris buns and sit at the counter. Father was happy just staring at the air. And I was content too, for I didn't have to talk to him.

There was still odd days when he had clear moments; times when some splinter of his past would come back to him. A shadow would cross his face at times like this, and he'd stumble over his words to catch the' memory before it got away. One day he minded his First Holy Communion, and another day he minded his Ordination. But the times he minded most of all was deaths and funerals. And then he tried for all his might to forget them. Poor tortured soul.

146

I mind the very first morning we spent at Knockmaroon. I'd stuck my head round the corner of the door to see how he was doing. And I seen him waking out of his sleep. His eyes was opened wide, though his body lay still as a rock on the bed. I watched his eyelids twitch, like he was in pain, as he tried to recover some splinter of his life. Then they went still again, like he was dead.

The first thing to be done that day, and every day after, was get the Mass out of the road. We had an oratory, of course, seeing as Father couldn't go out of the house to say Mass. It was in the room next to mine. All Father's garments from the chapel and anything else he needed to hold the sacraments was kept in here. During the time him and me was the-gether at Knockmaroon, I served as the sacristan, altar-boy and the entire congregation too, most of the time. For few people would walk the distance to our house when there was a chapel nearer-by in the town. Knockmaroon minded me on Bethel House where chapel and house and workplace was all under one roof and we didn't have to put up with outsiders pestering us. I knew enough by now to dress Father in the right garments and pick the proper prayers for the day. And, seeing as he couldn't read any more, I had to read the prayers as well, including the Gospel. That was the only rule him and me ever broke so long as we were saying the Mass; saying the Gospel, I mean. I was even particular to wear a headscarf, though, as I says, Father and me was nearly always on our own.

I preferred the Mass when it was just Father and me by ourselves. Indeed, I didn't want people in the house at no time, no matter what their business was. I might've known there'd aye be some busy-body or do-gooder barging in when they were least wanted. But I never give them no innings. I learned quick how to give them the cold shoulder without being downright ignorant. For I was sick of having to put up with people simply because I was a priest's maid. What right had people to stick their noses in my business anyway, or Father's either? Father didn't have nothing to do with the parish. So I didn't see why the parish should expect anything off him. And I wasn't interested in conversation. God, what I would've given to be invisible in them days. My main worry was Father would misbehave himself when somebody was in the house. It didn't bother me he'd embarrass somebody in the parish. What did bother me was the Bishop finding out. Then where would I be? The only people I could stand to see in them days was Tim and this wee spastic youngster that used to come in to talk to Father. Otherwise I felt under siege. Everybody else put in on me. The problem was, you see, I couldn't talk straight to any of them. None of them knew how bad Father really was and I wasn't going to tell them neither. It wasn't for my own sake alone, I didn't say. As I seen it, me talking about Father would've been like a wife talking about her husband behind his back and I never had no time for women who did that sort of thing. I couldn't even talk to Patsy—that was Father Jack's maid—for she was slow. There was another reason I didn't want people in. I'd got used to having the place to myself. And, unlike the way things was in Derry, I could tidy up or not if I liked. For Father was no longer in any state to complain.

In spite of me though, the parish took Father to its heart. Give a crowd like that a collar and they'll kneel down and worship. There was aye somebody or other calling to see what they could do. Nothing was too much for Father; or for me neither. I used these offers where they suited me. And, before long, I had the same set up here I had in Derry, with somebody aye willing to run errands for me or take me anywhere I wanted. Some Sundays, the local headmaster and his wife would offer to take Father on an outing to "get him off my hands," as they says. They'd take him to the Ness Woods or some other beauty spot in the vicinity. Not that Father ever knew where he was, or cared for that matter. It aye struck me as a terrible waste for there was plenty other old men and women in the parish—and them had their wits about them—that would've appreciated the outing far more than Father ever did. But nobody never offered to take them out; the reason being none of them was priests or nuns.

I know now, looking back, I was spoiled by the people roundabout. They were far too good to me. Indeed, I depended that much on one man to take out the bin for me, I never noticed one day he forgot. And a whole swarm of rats gathered round the rubbish. It was only when one of the beasts got inside the house I discovered what had happened. I was scared stiff on my own account, of course. (I never could abide pests.) But I was scared as well for fear Father would reach for the thing. He'd no more sense. So I called in Father Jack to get rid of the animal.

Father Jack turned up, like the fire-brigade, in minutes, horn tooting, and a load of clerical students in the back. The three young deacons he had visiting was local boys from the parish. It was odd to see boys that young all dressed up in black, like undertakers. But if the smiles on their faces was anything to go by, they didn't look any the worse for it. And they had a whale of a time, trying to corner the beast. The sound was in the house that night, the laughter and jollity, made me sad for it minded me of the days I worked for Father at the start. In them days he aye had young people about him and the place was teeming with life.

While the lads was hunting the beast, Father Jack stood

back and kept them going. "Jesus, Mary and Joseph," he kept swearing every time the animal got away, and rolled his eyes to Heaven. This was the first time I'd seen him since he delivered Father and me. And it was the first real chance I had to see if the country had made any change on him. Of course, he was drinking as heavy as ever. Miracles wasn't rife about Dungiven in them days. Not but his spirits was high, no matter how much drink he had in him. He'd aye been a big man but he was even bigger since leaving Derry. Dungiven obviously agreed with him—or with his stomach. And he still slouched his hips like John Wayne. Now, I'll tell you this about Father Jack. He had a manliness about him I rarely noticed in any other priest. Even God, it seems, hadn't the power to put that out of him. He threw his arm about me that night. "My money's on the rat, Brigid," he says. "What do you think?"

After an hour clowning around, the lads cornered the animal behind a sofa in the living room. But when they pulled away the sofa, glory be to God, the animal wasn't there, and there wasn't sight nor sign of it anywhere. Dumb beast as it was, it had managed to get the better of them. And Father Jack was mad as hell. Like a man on a mission, he flew off to the parochial house straight away and come back armed with poison and a trap. None of the rest of us could figure out in the meantime what had happened the animal. Flynn, the smallest lad, says it was "a miracle" though none of the other lads was inclined to agree with him.

My head was in that much of a spin that night with all the excitement, I couldn't say my prayers in peace, let alone go to sleep. Father wasn't able to rest neither and I could hear him roaming about upstairs. To make matters worse, the heat was terrible. Hot weather like this aye brought Father out at his worst. So I thought I'd better put him back in his bed where he'd be well out of harm's way. But, when I opened my room door, he was standing outside, wearing nothing at all. Not a stitch, I mean. I got the fright of my life. And all he could say was the heat was killing him. He reached for me round the neck and starting crying and complaining. Though I'd lived with the man for more than thirty years by now, he was a terrible stranger to me that night. Still and all, I did what I had to do— I was well used to that now—and got him back to his bed.

As if this wasn't enough for one night, I come back to my room to find the rat was in there with me. From the way it was carrying on, I figured it must've eaten some of the poison Father Jack put down; for it was writhing round like the devil, and kicking its heels in the air. It was more than I could stomach to look at it. So I come out of the room again and locked the door after me. It was dead at the foot of the bed when I went in again in the morning. That was the same morning I found Father sitting on the edge of the bed—his own bed, not mine—with blood gushing from his hands. Like the idiot he was, he'd taken the statue of the Virgin to bed with him and broken her head off in the middle of the night. And now some of the splinters of delph was lodged in his hands. He held his hands out for me to look at. A terrible sight he looked, too, between this and the shape of him. His hair was sticking out where I'd hacked it with the scissors. He wouldn't sit still for me to cut it, and it was all matted at the back where he lay on it when it was wet. He didn't look the same as usual neither. He wasn't wearing his usual troubled look. (At least that would've suggested there was something going on in his head.) Instead he was wearing this idiotic, pop-eyed grin which proved, clear as day, he hadn't a mind worth talking about any more. Then, for the first time, I knew I was dealing with a living corpse. I locked my bedroom door every night after that, you may be sure.

The people that caused me the most heartache during this time was, of course, the Bishop and Father's relatives. Like he used to do when I was working for Father in the beginning, Bishop Cleary would land in without a word to me. You'd think he'd have had the decency to call me first. But no. Not him. If you ask me, he did it deliberately; to catch me out and see what state Father was really in. But I was ready for him when he come, like the vestal virgins in the parable. He never give over quizzing me, neither. The way he was acting—sticking his nose in everywhere—you'd think he owned the place. Not that I was in any position to complain for he was paying the rent. Still and all, I don't think money give him the right to walk over me the way he did. He was that jealous, too. He acted like Father was his property. He was determined to get Father away from me the first real chance he got, if you ask me. All he needed was an excuse. And, if he couldn't prise him away, then he was determined to make life Hell for me. Which he did. It was his stupid notion I take the Lenten Station every year. That's when Mass is said in some house in the parish instead of the chapel. Imagine! And me with a sick man on my hands!

Whenever I knew Ronan and Miriam was coming, I give Father extra medicine so he'd behave himself. (In small doses the medicine never done nothing for him as far as I could see.) I was prepared for them the same way I was prepared for the Bishop. But, one day, the medicine didn't work and Father made a pass at Miriam. He held on to her that hard, Ronan had to separate them in the end. Miriam ordered me into the kitchen. She wasn't going to talk about a thing like sex in front of her husband. Lord, no!

"What exactly is going on in this house?" says she to me.

Just for badness, I pretended I didn't know what she was talking about.

"Don't think you can hide anything from me," says she, "I know what you're really like. It's not decent, a woman like you looking after Father Mann in the state he's in."

"Keep your wicked thoughts to yourself, Miriam Mann," I says to her. "You can't go telling tales to Father now."

God, but Miriam looked ugly when her temper was up. (Not that she was much to write home about at the best of times.) I could've ripped the hair out of her head that minute, the mood I was in. But I kept my hands to myself and my tongue in my teeth.

"You and me never seen eye to eye," Miriam says. And she took a stride towards me. But, at the same time, Ronan appeared in the kitchen door.

"I'm tormented with women's tongues," he says. And he glares at Miriam for all his worth. "You're not to breathe another word of this."

So what Father done was never mentioned after that. It's my opinion, Ronan wouldn't let Miriam mention it for Father was his brother, after all. And you know what they say about blood and water.

CHAPTER SIX

I'm not perfect, I know. None of God's creatures is. But nobody never had no reason to call me lazy, though by the carry on of the Bishop, you'd think I was living the life of Reilly. The fact of the matter is, after eleven years taking the Lenten Station, I was worn out. It was a desperate trial every time, for I never knew if Father was going to behave himself, or if the Bishop was going to see how things really was and give me my walking papers. Year after year, I pleaded with him to get somebody else to do the job instead of me. But he was that pig-headed. He says that keeping Father minded what a Station was would be good for him. And it would be good for the parishioners too, he says. It would keep them minded who Father really was. No harm to the Bishop; he had his job to do. But I'd had up to my teeth of it. I didn't see why the other women in the parish shouldn't pull their weight as well as me. There was plenty dying to do it, I know, for a Station was the best excuse going to buy a new suite of furniture or new carpets. Take Maggie Smith, for instance. She was a terrible house-proud woman and would jump at the chance to show her place off. Tim told me that before I come the women was tearing one another's hair out for the opportunity. Father Jack had to come between them many's a time, he says. But none of them was going to come up against Father and me, least not so long as the Bishop was calling the shots.

I mind as well the last Station ever Father and me took. It happened about Easter-time which was busy enough without this added on top of it. Just like me, I left everything till the last minute for the Station was late in the day on account the Bishop was attending a Confirmation in Faughanvale the same morning. Only that morning itself, I got round to making the place presentable. (People expect a clean house at a Station.) I was polishing the pictures belonging to Father which was hanging up round the sitting room: Father as an altar boy, Father at his Ordination, the class from Maynooth, Father at his first Mass, and so on. Poor soul. He was sitting in the room with me at the same time and staring into empty space. The pictures meant nothing to him any more. He wouldn't have known himself from Peter, God help him. I stopped a minute at the picture of him with Pope John Paul that was taken the time the Pope was visiting Ireland. The Pope-mobile was in the background and thousands of heads was crushing to have a look at His Holiness. God, I mind that day well. You never seen a crowd like it. The Pope drew a bigger crowd than ever was seen at Slane or Lisdoonvarna. That was a proud moment for Father. He looked fresh in the face in that picture, and flushed and excited the way he looked the very first day ever I seen him. I breathed on the glass and wiped it with the duster. Father's face shone out like a light. But my heart sunk in my chest as I made my way round the rest of the pictures: Father's farewell to the parish, the Bishop presenting him with a gold chalice. Them times was burned into my memory like a brand, not to mention all the misery that come along with them. And all Father could do was sit there, like an idiot, and stare at nothing. He didn't have to live with his memories any more. Only me had to live with them and they were all his memories.

It was about this same time he got the bad habit of going back to bed after I dressed him for the day. Three times already that morning I'd had to rise him. In the end, I turned the lock in the bedroom door in case he'd sneak in again unknown to me. For he could still be fly enough when the fancy took him. Sleeping was the last thing on my mind on the other hand. Since getting up that morning, my head hadn't given me a minute's peace. Places and faces from the past—some of them I hadn't thought about in twenty years—kept coming back to me. And they come that fast, I couldn't make head nor tail of them. All I could do was keep myself distracted. Not that I had much choice with a hundred odd people expected in the house any minute and the cobwebs still hanging from the rafters.

I was glazing the hot-cross buns in the kitchen when Tim come in. Now Tim would never be seen dead at Mass, 'specially not at our house. Still he come at other times to give me a hand whenever he thought it might be needed. He'd tempered a fair bit since that first day Father and me met him at the gate. I give him one of the buns was finished into his hand.

"Need anything doing, Brigid?" says he to me and he left to one side the hazel rods he made a habit of carrying about with him. Divining water was a hobby of his, you see. People was aye getting him in as well to discover things was lost that they couldn't get their hands on any other way.

God love him, Tim was a good soul. I asked him to keep an eye on Father while I changed my clothes. For he was a dab hand at looking after him. In fact, he was the only one I trusted to look after Father any more; not since Father got that bad anyway. Tim would come in some days, when he had an hour, and take him into the garden to give me a rest. Though I don't think Matty was pleased for she give me a dirty look any time I run into her in the supermarket. That particular morning of the Station, I was dying for someone to talk to. And I could aye talk to Tim. I couldn't ever talk to anybody else the same way. It was Tim taught me to say my piece without feeling scared or guilty any more. I could say the things I didn't like about Father, for instance the sick smell on his breath, or the scurf under his toenails. I didn't like the fine slimy paste he ate neither. (Everything he took had to be put through the blender now for he couldn't eat solid food any more.) It looked like baby food. And he'd squeeze it back through his lips when he didn't like the taste of it. I couldn't stomach that neither. But I could say all these things now. So I told Tim how angry I was at having to take the Station another year.

"You did your share," Tim agreed with me. "Let some other woman do it next year."

That was good of him, bolstering me up like that. And him had his own troubles. Tim wasn't happy, I knew. Not by a far cry.

"Joan'll be over to give you a hand," he says, "as soon as she gets the cows milked."

Joan was his youngest and still lived with him and her mother. He had another daughter who went to England to have an abortion and was never heard tell of after that. Tim himself never breathed her name in my hearing. He had a son as well—a bad one. But Joan, God love her, was a good hard wee worker and not afraid to get her hands dirty, not like some. She'd bend over backwards to accommodate you. I aye had a soft spot for Joan. Apart from being a good soul in herself, she had Tim's good looks and his kindness to boot. And she doted on her da, though Tim could be awful sore on her sometimes. Nothing she did was ever enough for him. It aye seemed to me the nicer people was to Tim the harder he was on them, and Joan was no exception. God, but that man could be contrary.

"What's wrong this morning, Brigid?" he says to me, for he could see there was more on my mind than just the Station.

"My head's been going round since the morning," I says to him, "and I can't make head nor tail of it. Past, present and future; they're all jumbled the-gether. I've been minding that much, more than any soul should have to put up with in one life."

"Never mind, Brigid," says he to me. "We all have days like that. I put no pass on them myself—just turn my mind on the beasts or something. That's the thing about having a farm. It keeps your mind off things it does no good dwelling on."

"What does your mind dwell on, Tim?" I says to him.

"On the wife," says he, "and my sisters. Vera died of cancer last year, you know. And Fannie went to be a nun in the Far East. I haven't seen her now in nearly twenty years."

I asked him about Josie. Josie was the youngest and the one his Joan took after. And, if I minded rightly, Tim had aye had a soft spot for her when they were youngsters. Not but he looked depressed when I mentioned her name now.

"Oh, Josie," he says. "She done nothing with her life. She's in and out of Gransha Hospital most of the time.

"Does she have a family?" I says to him.

"None of them married," says he. Whatever was eating him, he ripped the cross off the hot cross bun.

"But you married," I says.

"Aye," he says. And the way he laughed give me the impression he wished he hadn't. Of course Tim would never say anything, but I knew rightly he wasn't happy with Matty. You see, Matty was a plain, down to earth wee woman, a proper

158

farmer's wife with a shape to go with it. She minded me on a duck, the way she walked, she was that flat-footed. And she was a good ten years older than Tim and looked every day of it. But I told you that before. As far as I know, her and Tim never went out the-gether. Tim just went to the pictures on his own, the same way he used to do. Old habits die hard, as the saying goes.

It was funny, Tim saying that about his wife and sisters. When I was worked up it was usually my own lot run round in my mind, too: my ma, God rest her soul, and my da; and Dympna and Michael; and the nuns and priests, of course. That day I couldn't get my da out of my head. I knew him to be a man with a wild temper and it bothered me I might take after him. I says as much to Tim. But Tim looked at me like I was having him on. "Wouldn't you be afraid if you had a killer's blood coursing round your veins?" says I.

"Aye," says he, a bit reluctant. Though he took me serious after that and asked how come my ma and da didn't get on.

"The fighting started before Michael was born," I says to him. "My da couldn't stand my ma being pregnant. He wanted her to stay the wee girl he married, you see."

Joan come in at that minute. God love her! She had a pile of fresh tea-towels in her hand, and she started cleaning up the breakfast things that was sitting on the sink. Nothing went beyond Joan. So I went on telling Tim about my ma and da.

Says I, "Things didn't get better when my ma made plain Michael and Dympna was to be brought up Catholics. (I wasn't around at this time, you see.) My da tried locking her in Sundays, during Mass time. But she only went out later in the week and took Michael and Dympna with her."

"Matty and me had the same problem," Tim says. At the same time, I noticed, he took a sideways glance at Joan. "I had to let her have her way in the end. Now all my youngsters is Catholics, God help them."

"Now Da," Joan scowls at him. "My ma wouldn't need to hear you saying that."

"But y'r not going to breathe a word, now, are you Joan?" Tim says to her with a big grin on his face from ear to ear.

Joan says nothing more. (Where was the point as far as Tim was concerned?) And I went on with what I was saying.

Tim looked troubled when I told him about my da being in Gransha. "It's scary, that," he says, "the way one bout of badness can change your whole life."

"That's why I like to stay in charge," I says. "But days like the-day, I have the terrible temptation to tell people where to go."

I wasn't telling Tim a lie neither for I couldn't stand people fighting over Father the way they did. The Bishop, the people in the parish and Ronan and Miriam; they were like the soldiers fighting for Our Lord's garments after the Crucifixion. All I wanted was a bit of peace.

Tim hung around a good while that morning. It wasn't on my account, mind you. He just didn't want to go home for Matty was on the rampage over some cattle he'd forgot to worm. That kind of thing was all Matty ever thought about. Tim wasn't one for the pub neither. So ours was the only place he had to go.

As early as half past nine, women from the parish started coming in with extra rugs and chairs and delph; anything to get in with the clergy. The place was crawling with them. They were the same lot cleaned the chapel, counted the Mass-money and run the local socials. You know the breed yourself—the kind that bully a body with kindness. This day they were arsing

160

about like horses and getting under my feet. Honest to God, you'd think from the way they were carrying on I didn't know how to tie my own shoe-laces. They seemed to think I was doting at my age and going senile along with Father. If there's anything gets on my nerves it's people treating me like an infant. Maggie Smith was the worst. She started re-arranging the furniture and checking the tea-cups for stains. In the end, I flipped. I was trying to find a space on the kitchen table for the tons of baking they'd brought when my temper got the better of me. And I tipped the table over. At the same time, I let out a mighty scream. Tim come running in from the back shed where he'd gone to get a smoke. And Joan, God bless her, threw her arms round me. The busy-bodies just stood there in the meantime, and gawped at me like I'd committed a terrible sacrilege.

There was cream buns and flans everywhere. All Tim could do was laugh. The women didn't think it was a laughing matter though, for one of them off and phoned Father Jack right away. "She's having a breakdown," I heard her telling him, while the rest of them stood and gawped at me. "Would you like a photo?" I says to them. With that they started whispering ninety to the dozen among themselves. Not one of them had a kind word to say to me. I got my own back when Father Jack appeared, though.

"I, for one, can be doing without as many cream cakes," says he, and he patted his big belly.

Joan cleaned up the mess. And everything was back to normal by the time the Bishop appeared. Them same women that hadn't a word to say to Father before, started fawning and fussing over him now. Anything for a show—anything to impress the Bishop. If I had a penny for every time one of them says, "Poor pet," I'd be a rich woman. One even tried to tell the Bishop she thought Father was lucky. I could have killed her. That day I wised up. I had no more illusions people was doing things for Father and me. All they ever thought about was themselves. They just used Father, poor mindless soul that he was, and they used me the same way. It was a sin.

After the state I was in, Tim and Joan says they'd stay with me. The three of us stuck the-gether; the three of us, that is, and Father Jack. Tim offered to keep an eye on Father Mann which let me look after people was coming in.

And Joan helped by peeling the spuds for the priest's dinner. A Station was a right ordeal for it could go on till all hours of the night or morning providing the priests had enough to eat and drink. The confessions come first. I usually set aside the front room for this so as people could queue up in the hall. Though I hated the way they rubbed their backsides on the wall. It tore the wallpaper. The blessing of the beads and medals and anything else needed blessing come after that. This day, the Bishop must've sprinkled a gallon of holy water round the place. There was a terrible rattling and rustling of paper. I still can't credit the stupidity of some people. They think a blessing won't go through a paper bag. The Mass, as Father said it, usually took an hour and a half. Then there was tea and biscuits for the congregation. This was the time people grappled with one another for a few words with the Bishop. The worst part for me was the priests' dinner which come after this, for I was out of the way of entertaining a crowd of priests on a regular basis. All the priests in the parish and any visiting priests had to be invited whether they were taking part in the Station or not. And I was expected to lay on a three course meal for them, not to mention all the wine and sherry and whiskey they could drink. It took me a whole day to do the shopping and another day to make it ready. I'm not complaining, though. Joan, God love her, had helped me out the night before. And everything was ready except the spuds.

I was sorting out a couple of youngsters was fighting for first place in the queue to Confession when the Bishop come up to me. His first words to me was aye the same. "And how's the patient today, Brigid," he'd say. But this day he didn't ask about Father Mann. He lowered his voice to a whisper instead and asked me if I knew where Father Jack had disappeared to—like he was the genie of the lamp or something. Of course, I knew right well where Father Jack was. He was in the kitchen, helping himself to the brandy. But I wasn't going to tell the Bishop that.

It was a fighting match trying to get Father ready for Mass. He was that contrary, he wouldn't wear the white vestment he was supposed to wear and demanded to wear the purple one in its place. No amount of coaxing or cajoling would win him over. By rights, I would've needed three heads and three pairs of hands to keep everything going that day. Father Jack hadn't put in an appearance since the Bishop was looking for him, so I thought I better have a word with him. He was still in the kitchen, wouldn't you know, blethering away to Joan who was up to her elbows in the kitchen sink.

"Why aren't you courting, Joan?" he was asking her when I come on him.

The kind of Joan, she kept him going. "I never found the man was good enough for me," she tells him.

But Father Jack was her match. "You're too fond of y'r da. That's what's wrong with you, Joan McFaul," he says.

"You're right there." Joan smiled a big, innocent smile at him.

It was then I says the Bishop was on the prowl, and told

Father Jack he better look out for himself. First things first, he tucked the brandy bottle under the kitchen sink, for fear anyone else would finish it on him, and put a polo mint in his mouth. "So long as he doesn't smell me before the Consecration," he says. "I can put it down to altar wine after that." And then he started to curse, the same way he always did when the Bishop was hounding him. "That Jesus was one lucky bugger—had red wine for blood coursing round his veins," he says. "No wonder he got himself crucified." For a priest, Father Jack come out with some rare things, and some not so rare things that he had no more business saying. "You're looking spruce, the-day, Brigid Keen," he says to me. But before he could rave any further, I shoved him out of the kitchen and told him to get changed. For the Station Mass was aye concelebrated.

"God, but y'r a pushy woman," he scowls at me. "The Almighty has all the time in the world, surely he can wait a minute for me."

"I'm not worried about the Almighty," I says. "It's Bishop Cleary I'm worried about."

"Ahh! Put no pass on him," says he. "He's all wind and no matter."

Between roasting beef and burning candle wax, there was the oddest jumble of smells in the house that day. The altar looked gorgeous, heaped up with gladioli, and the geraniums I'd picked from the garden in the morning.

Them that had come early was chanting the Rosary in the living room. As soon as this was over, Father O'Kane, who was a right, religious wee priest and Father Jack's sidekick, launched into the Stations of the Cross. He had his own portable set which he brought round the Station houses during Lent. Without as much as by your leave, he set them up all over the house and made a procession round them one by one. I'll tell you something now. I never did like the Stations of the Cross. All that talk of stripping and lashing. They're written in such a way gets people all worked up. But they only ever managed to make me cringe. I never could stand the way some people, priests included, gloated over them. It's sick, if you ask me.

There was a good turn-out that day. Of course, Miriam and Ronan was there. And Damon. He'd just got his exams and was looking down his nose at everybody. When it come the time for Mass, all I had to do was set Father behind the altar, and, like a youngster on a sleigh, he managed the rest of the way on his own. No effort was needed.

"In the name of the Father and of the Son and of the Holy Spirit." The rigmarole had started and I took my place in the kitchen door where I could see better what was going on. Father Jack says the Antiphon. "Grant we beseech Thee, almighty God, that we who are continually afflicted by reason of our excesses, may be delivered through the passion of Thine only begotten Son." And I says the tract. Father managed to get through the Gloria, the Creed and the Prayers of the Faithful, no bother. But when it come to the Gospel, Father Jack upset the apple-cart by asking Tim to do the reading. He was that through-going, he did it for badness, I know. "Let's give Brigid's mouth a rest," he says to Tim. Poor Tim. He couldn't rightly say no without a fight. Even at the best of times, he was a shy man. And it was painful to watch him standing up there, all red with embarrassment. He stumbled over words that was strange to him and ran the sentences all the-gether. "The Jews said to Jesus: Do not we say well, that Thou art a Samaritan and hast a devil? Jesus answered: I have not a devil."

Father reached the Offertory without a hitch and sat down

while the basket, for the money, was handed round. He listened till he heard the last coin clink, then got up again and started the Consecration. In the eleven years since he was taken ill, I'd never known him get the Mass wrong once, not even them times after he'd missed a night's sleep and was more through-other than usual. People says it was a miracle. It was during the Preface to the Eucharist I noticed something was wrong with him for he stopped dead in his tracks and started to stare at me. The stare buckled into a shame-faced look, and I urged him on another bit. But he stopped a second time. By now, the people was shuffling round in their seats and signing and whispering to one another. They looked at me and they looked at the Bishop to see what was going on. Only when Father let out a whimper did I know, for certain, what the matter was. He'd wet himself. Big tears was streaming down his face and he stared at the pool of water round his feet. But before I had time to come to his assistance, that young upstart, Father O'Kane, took the foreroad of me. He rushed him out of the room, leaving Father Jack to say the rest of the Mass. Father Jack stayed well round the front of the altar, not near the back where Father had been. He couldn't walk on water, he says. Though me nor nobody else that was there was in any humour for his jokes that day.

The looks on some people's faces was very odd when they discovered what had happened. They seen the miracle wasn't a miracle, and they looked scared and disappointed, not to mention embarrassed. Some of them even looked to me for re-assurance in Father's place. May God forgive me, but I didn't have no time for any of them that day. My only concern was Father. When I got to his room, I discovered that young scut, Father O'Kane, hadn't lifted a finger to help him. You think he might've cleaned him up, at least. But, knowing him, he likely thought a job like that too low for priests' hands. The Communion was all but over by the time I come back to the Mass again. Father O'Kane held on a minute, thinking I wanted to go. I didn't though. Leastwise, not to him, I didn't. It wouldn't have been right anyway in the mood I was in.

The first chance he got me on my own, the Bishop cornered me. "You haven't been straight with me, Brigid," he says. "You led me to believe Father Mann could say Mass very well."

I didn't know how to answer him and my knees was like jelly under me. All I could think was they were going to take Father away from me. "I looked after Father thirty-three years," I says. "And I can look after him the rest of his days."

"That's out of the question," the Bishop says back, and he steered me into the drawing room in front of him. Miriam and Ronan was there already and waiting on us by all appearances. I could see the glint in Miriam's eye.

"We're going to take Father away," she says. "He should have been in a home long ago."

Ronan glowered at her. He didn't like her taking the foreroad of him like that. But before he could make his presence felt, Damon and Father O'Kane appeared on the scene.

I felt surrounded. All I could do was hold my hands tight between my knees (they were shaking that hard) while Bishop Cleary scowled about how much I'd let him down. Not one of the others come to my defence in any way. "The wicked have wrought upon my back." These words from the psalm, come into my mind. Nor could I defend myself neither, for I didn't have the education nor the background to argue with the likes of them. I took a long look round all the faces. This lot have the clout, I says to myself, and I have none. My nails was cutting hard into the hearts of my hands by this time.

"There's more to consider than you and Father Mann," the Bishop says. "I have to think about those people out there. And they want to know that everything's OK."

"But everything is OK," I pleaded with him.

He was determined, though. "We can't have a repeat of this incident we had here today," he says. "And now that Father Mann can't say Mass any more, there is no reason to have him in the community."

Says I, "He wanted to live with me."

"Your job's done, Brigid," he says. "Go out and enjoy yourself."

Enjoy myself! What in God's name did he take me for?

"Enjoy myself?" I says. "With who? On what? I love Father."

Well, you should've seen the Bishop's face when I says that. His jaw dropped a good two inches. Says he, "I won't hear another word of this," and he glowers at me like I'd just committed sacrilege.

"Only a couple of stragglers come to Mass anyway," I says.

Then he took a real deep breath. And I could see him working himself up, like an actor, to use the soft touch on me. "Consider Father Mann in all of this, Brigid," he says to me in a real gentle voice. "If he was fit to judge for himself, is this what he would want?"

I was still pleading my case, though to no end, when Father Jack come in on us. "What's all the confabulation?" says he in a big loud voice. "By the look on your faces, somebody just committed a mortal sin. Ah Fintan..." He aye addressed the Bishop by his first name. "Let the man die in peace. Let Brigid here take care of him."

"He's not in control. He should be in professional care," the Bishop says.

"You mean you don't like him living with Brigid in the state he's in. Isn't that it?" says Father Jack.

The Bishop was fuming. "That's enough. I'll have no more argument," he says.

But he couldn't silence Father Jack. "The way you talk a body'd think the old bastard was living in sin."

Grabbing Father Jack by the arm, the Bishop dragged him out of the room. I overheard the words "drunk" and "filthy mind" from where I was standing near the door jamb. Words like that sounded rare coming from the Bishop with his lovely voice.

"Well, I never!" Miriam says, and she looked at Ronan and Damon in turn to back her up. But Ronan was in no mood to humour her. He'd heard more than he wanted to hear that day.

"Father Mann needs professional care," Damon says in a slow, affected drawl. "I think we ought to ring the Nazareth House and make arrangements right away."

The Bishop agreed with this plan whenever he come back into the room.

"But what am I going to do now?" I says to him.

"You're a free agent, Brigid," he says. "You do as you please."

"But what am I going to do?" I asked him another time, for I didn't think he got the gist of what I was saying to him the first time.

"That's up to you, Brigid," he says, and from the way he was shifting from one foot to the other I could see he was losing patience with me.

May God forgive him! I'd just lost the man I spent the last thirty-three years with, and my home and job into the bargain. And he didn't have two minutes to spend on me.

That same afternoon Father was taken to the Nazareth

House. The priests seen him off, then come back in for their dinner like nothing had happened. Not one of them, except Father Jack of course, had any notion the agony I was in. They didn't only expect me to provide a dinner but to do it with a smile as well. "Cheer up," the Bishop says to me a couple of times. "It'll never happen." He was very lucky I didn't throw the dinner in his face.

Getting to see Father was terrible difficult. For, seeing as I wasn't a priest's maid, properly speaking, lifts wasn't easy to come by any more; not the way they used to be anyway. The sacristan did give me a lift into Derry the first couple of mornings, mind you. And I come back by the late bus. That way I got to spend the whole day with Father, providing the wee nurses would let me. And to give them their dues, they weren't bad about it in the beginning. None of them made me feel I was under their feet nor nothing, the way some nurses can. And they even give me tea.

The third day it was, Father forgot my name. You may know how I felt if you ever had a relative go senile on you. It nearly broke my heart. I felt as if I didn't exist so long as Father didn't know my name any more. Still I kept my spirits up for his sake. I took him wee things I knew he liked till the Sister put a stop to it. She says he had a strict diet he had to stick to. How else did I expect him to stay well, she says? As if I was going to do anything to harm him. I'll tell you now, I couldn't live on the stuff they fed him in there. Maybe it was good for him. Who am I to say? But there can't have been much joy in it.

The nurses soon got tired of me, the way people will after the novelty wears off. And I was just allowed to see Father a couple of hours in the day. One of them—a wee Nurse Friel, it was—says they were sending me away for my own good. Of course I could've complained. But I didn't dare for fear they'd send me away all the-gether. And I couldn't stand to lose Father a second time.

As I says, the sacristan give me a lift in the beginning. Then one day, she says she couldn't make it. And the next, she didn't turn up at all. Anybody else I asked says they were too busy or they hadn't got the petrol. One man says to me his car was broke down, though I seen the car on the road an hour later. I had no choice in the end but to take the bus, which meant hanging around Derry till the nurses let me in. They didn't like me coming till after lunch. Still, they let me stay till five when Father got his tea, and that filled the day for me. I don't know what I'd have done otherwise.

The self-same day Father left, Ronan and Damon come to take his things away, or keep an eye on the men they hired to do the job for them. (You never seen Ronan or Damon getting their hands dirty. Not them.) Damon come armed with a big long list of everything should be in the place. Where he got it from I don't know, unless he made it up himself when he was visiting earlier. If as much as a spoon was missing, he had me hunting the house till I found it. I swear to God he wouldn't give me a minute's peace. He had me screening for this and that, things I hadn't set eyes on in twenty years. I had to watch my few odds and ends in the process for fear he'd run away with them as well. Not but most of the stuff was in the place belonged to Father, except a few things—a cooker, a table and a couple of chairs—that was there when we moved in. Damon took the lot. But, if you ask me, he would've done right to give some of the things away; the things that was worn out especially. I knew a couple of poor families in the parish could've been doing rightly with them. Ronan wouldn't listen

171

though. This wasn't all. I would've liked some wee thing of Father's myself, one of his books or something, to mind him by. But Damon offered nothing and I knew better than to ask.

With Father gone, I was at a terrible loss what to do with myself; Sundays in particular, when I couldn't get a bus and had to stay at home alone. I say home. But Knockmaroon wasn't my home any more. It was only ever rented for Father's benefit and the lease run out in three weeks' time. I told anybody that asked, I was moving in with my sister. Of course, I hadn't any intention of going to Dympna's. If nothing else, her Charlie wouldn't have me. And I wasn't going to stay where I wasn't wanted. The way I was feeling them days, I couldn't bring myself to look for some place else to live, even I had the rent to pay for it—which I hadn't. And I was in no better mood to go looking for a job. The very thought of going out of the house to work struck the fear of God into me. I'd worked that long at home, you see, I was spoiled with it.

At that same time I didn't want to see or talk to anyone, not even Tim. He'd come to the door looking for me but I kept the curtains pulled and pretended I wasn't in. I spent most of the time sulking, like a wean kicking at a door after it's been put out for being bad. When I wasn't hiding under the bedclothes, I was boiling mad, at the Bishop, in particular, for dropping me like a hot brick and leaving me stranded the way he did. At least he might've got me some place else to live, I says to myself. I was angry at the people round me as well. Take the sacristan and her husband for instance. They promised the day Father left they'd come and take me to Mass. But they never did. I seen their big flash Volvo pass the front gate the Sunday after. Children's heads was bouncing round in the back seat and the sacristan herself was sitting up in the front, all dressed up to the ninety-nines. There wasn't a soul to take out the dust-bin for me neither, and nobody to keep the weeds down in the garden. One day the milkman scratched the date off the milk bottle and palmed me off with stale milk. The stuff was that rotten you couldn't put it in your tea. You may be sure this kind of thing never happened so long as Father was living with me. I had fallen in the world, as they say. But after three weeks blaming other people I realised in the end it was up to me to pick myself up. Nobody else cared. Nobody else was responsible.

Father Jack disappeared about the same time Father went away. The word was he'd gotten sick all of a sudden. But I had it from his maid, on the quiet, he was off somewhere drying out. The Bishop's orders!

The week before the lease was up, Tim come to hang the "To Let" sign across the road. He hung it on a tall tree. There wasn't a whiff of wind that night. And I could hear his hammering—tap, tap, tap—like he was hammering the nails in my coffin lid.

———◦———

CHAPTER SEVEN

It was Bishop Cleary's fault I never went to Holy Communion after Father went away. For he says I was greedy when I asked to stay on longer at Knockmaroon, when all I wanted was a roof over my head, the same as any woman would after her man was gone. Then there might've been something to his story. I see that now. For our Dympna says to me many's a time, I was never satisfied. Whatever it was, I aye wanted more than I had in front of me. Take, for instance, the time I went through three whole boxes of communion hosts during one episode of *Neighbours*. God love the Bishop; he thought he was doing a roaring trade about Dungiven from the amount of the stuff I went through. And I never let on, neither, so he was nothing the wiser. Well, I was just the same about staying on at the house. I didn't want to budge even after the lease was up.

Let me tell you something now. Deprivation's a terrible thing. I never had a real home over my head, you see. And that made me hang on all the harder here. As I seen it, I was ousted early from the womb (on account of what my da did to my ma. And I come by caesarian, into the bargain). And I was ousted early from Bethel House when I went to work for Father. (I never had much of a youth to speak of.) Now they were ousting me from Knockmaroon before I was ready to go. Though the Bishop hadn't sent me strict notice to shift yet, I was expecting word any day.

It was only after I was rid of Father, I discovered I hadn't had a decent wink of sleep in over ten years; not since he got real bad anyway. I'd been keeping that sharp an eye on him, I hadn't been able to dream in peace. The mind needs some release and mine hadn't got none. All that sleeping and all that dreaming still had to be done. But it would have to wait a while longer, until I got myself another place at least. For I couldn't get to sleep in Knockmaroon any more. The place was that empty and eerie late at night it would scare the devil out of you between strange creaks and noises and shadows coming out of nowhere at me. I kept expecting a murderer to land in any minute. And I was feared stiff of ghosts into the bargain. Inside was full of dark corners and crannies for them to hide in, not to mention the dark barns and storehouses was outside. Every room I went into and every corner I turned round, I expected to run into some of the people lived and died in the house before Father and me come. I kept my eyes and ears peeled when I should've been sleeping at night. Night after night this vigil continued till, in the end, my nerves got the better of me. And I had to get in a wee cutty to stay with me. You mind the wee backward wean I says come in to talk to Father; well, her. And she stayed in the same bed with me. She wasn't any bother neither, for she come and went without a word. Her ma says that was one good thing about her. She didn't blether on the way some youngsters have a habit of doing. And she didn't have enough sense to be scared.

The time soon wore round till the first day of spring. It had slipped my mind to wind on the clock the night before, and I was doing it about dinner the following day when there come a knock on the door. From the sharp rap, I knew fine well it was Mrs Hussey, the "good neighbour" young Father O'Kane paid to

175

go round and pester people. This Mrs Hussey was a one woman charity, with nothing to give away foreby a sore head. And she give me plenty of them. For since I'd come down in the world, she'd put me on her list of poor unfortunates she called in on every week. The last time she called, she had the nerve to tell me I shouldn't shut myself away. Them was her words. As if it was any of her business. As if there was anyone in that parish I had a word to say to. She even tried to drag me to the bingo in the church hall the Sunday night of the big snow-ball. But I wouldn't give her the satisfaction. Her family was all grown up, you see, and her husband was retired. So when she couldn't lord it over the weans at home, she tried to lord it over people elsewhere. All I can say is, God help the poor souls had to put up with her, me included.

I knew it was no good trying to hide from this one. The kind she was, she'd stand on the doorstep till night unless you opened the door to her. The first time she come to see me, she went round and round the house, peering in the windows and banging on the doors. You talk about contrary. Well, that one took the biscuit. I had no choice but to let her in in the end. It was either that or crawl round the place on my hands and knees all day till she disappeared. This particular day she had another woman with her whose face I knew from years back in the Bishop's house. (When you see a face like that, from long ago, it makes you realise how old you are. This one had a sight more wrinkles, I can tell you.) Such a poker face you never seen. And she was wearing a pin-stripe suit, the kind men only used to wear in my day. She was holding a brief case tight under her oxter. Mrs Peters, her name was, though I noticed she wasn't wearing a ring. But that kind of thing was getting common, even in Derry. I can't mind the proper word for what she done now. But I know she looked after the Bishop's money for him.

I guessed right. She'd come to tell me to leave the house. The Bishop didn't have the bare face to tell me himself, so he sent a woman in his place. Can you beat it! Hiding behind a woman's skirts like that. He should've been ashamed of himself.

I asked the pair in and made them a cup of tea. Mrs Peters looked awful jittery, just sitting there while the kettle boiled and I laid the table. Still and all, I wasn't going to be put out of my own way of going, not for anyone, even her. I liked to lay the table the exact same way I did when Father was with me, though I'd little china left—only some odd cups I'd hid from Ronan when he was clearing the place. My table mattered as much to me as their altar did to the priests at Mass. Whenever I was done, I stood well back and made sure everything was in place. The digestives was all lined up even on the plate and the shortbread made a grand display. Mrs Hussey says the same thing she aye says when I set the cup of tea down in front of her. "It's always good to get tea in your house, Brigid," she says. "Nobody makes tea like a priest's maid any more." Not but she was right. The kind of women was going, most of them was too lazy to take the bag off the loaf let alone butter the bread for you. Nearly everywhere you went, you were likely to get nothing with the tea but the spoon, unless a priest or a teacher was in at the same time; in which case, you got the works. But I'd no time for this new-fangled way women had of doing things—or not doing them, to be more accurate. I didn't know what the world was coming to. Me, I took pride in laying a good table, and I made sure there was always something in the house for the tea. I swear, I couldn't've slept in my bed at night if there wasn't a packet of biscuits in the house. Dympna used to maintain a few youngsters under my feet would soon put that out of me. Then she maintained that about everything. If you ask me, her weans was her excuse for never lifting a hand. And another thing; she was jealous as well that I took the bother for other people. I didn't sit at the table myself that day or any day for that matter. The kind of me, I preferred to take a drop in my hand by the fire. Sitting at the table aye smothered me.

Mrs Peters was pulling in a chair when she sat down on something I'd thrown behind me. I have to confess, I'd gotten a bad habit of throwing things at my backside since Father went away. For there was rarely a soul in the house to see the way things was.

"Sorry," I says to her, and pulled whatever it was out from under her. A pair of Father's old long-johns, it was, that I'd left out to bring to him.

Mrs Peters went red in the face and started crumbling a Marie biscuit into her tea. She was the kind broke up her food instead of eating it. "And how is Father Mann these days?" she says.

I told her the plain truth. "Father's gone downhill awful fast since they took him away from me," I says. I noticed the looks passing between her and Mrs Hussey. The merest mention of Father made Mrs Hussey anxious as well. And I'll tell you why. Since leaving the parish, Father had dropped in the estimation of them same two-faced liars that called him an angel at the start. As far as any of them was concerned, he was now no more than a doating, done old man, like any other doating, done old man or woman in the Nazareth House. His needs was no longer being paid for by the Church, you see, and them same people knew it. (The Bishop and Father's family decided it cost too much to keep him private, and they handed him over to the

State instead.) Into the bargain, there was the wee matter of what happened at the Station. And being the tight-laced, tight-lipped kind they were, Mrs Hussey and her sort couldn't deal with this. (It doesn't do a priest no good at all to be seen to be human.) What happened that day brought home to them just how much Father needed me. I dressed him and fed him and cleaned up after him. Them was the bare facts and Mrs Hussey and her kind didn't like them very much. It wasn't proper, according to them, for a woman to be doing things like that for a priest. That day of the Station, I could see the pictures going through their minds. Then they'd also been caught out believing a miracle that wasn't a miracle after all. (I mean about Father saying the Mass.) And this looked bad for their faith. Of course they wanted rid of me for all the same reasons they wanted rid of Father. I was a sharp reminder of some home truths they preferred to forget. I was an embarrassment to them, if you want to put it that way.

The few things I owned, the lot of which I'd packed weeks before, was sitting in a pile in the corner of the room. Mrs Peters broke a digestive in half, then broke a corner off one of the halfs. She nodded at the pile of boxes. "And when will you be ready to leave?" she says.

"When do you want me to leave?" says I back to her. For I figured to myself she couldn't bare-faced ask me to go right away. And I clung on to any day there was in it. It hadn't passed my notice that, in spite of her hatchet face, Mrs Peters was inclined to take my side. I wasn't used making decisions into the bargain. In the past, you see, I'd aye waited to be told what to do and what not to do. And no one had told me yet to leave the house. If I'd been like many another up-to-date woman, I suppose, I would've jumped at the chance to start again on my own. But the very idea scared the living daylights out of me. I didn't dare picture the days and months ahead. Living for Father had been easy. I seen that much now. Living for myself was going to be the difficult part. And I didn't know if I could master it.

While Mrs Peters was looking up her diary, I mind, I spent the time going over the scars on my hands. No matter where I went or how long I lived, them scars would aye go with me, and they'd mind me of Father. They'd all come off the oven in the time I spent working for him. The long one on my inside forearm I got one day I was making a souffle. Father used to say if it was an inch lower it would've looked interesting—whatever that was supposed to mean. (Just like him. He was never satisfied with things being the way they were. He aye wanted them different.) The two dark scars in the hearts of my hands I got from gripping a hot bread-tray. And the one on the side of my forefinger, that come from scraping spuds day after day.

"What about next Sunday?" Mrs Peters says. "It will have to be next Sunday, in fact. The owner has some clients coming to look the place over on Monday night."

What could I say? I may not have many strengths but I know fate when it's staring me in the face. There's many a wife, I'm sure, has stayed in a bad marriage to avoid pulling up roots the way I was forced to pull up roots that day. Maybe I should've been grateful.

I looked from Mrs Peters to Mrs Hussey and back again, the way Jesus might've looked at the two thieves when he was crucified. Honest to God, between the pair of them, I didn't know where I was. Mrs Hussey had come to do me a good turn by all appearances, but I knew right well she couldn't wait to see the back of me. On the other hand, Mrs Peters had come to throw me out of the house. But, now she'd seen my predicament, she was sorry for me and disinclined to throw me out on the street. Then she had her orders, like me, and had to stick to them.

Mrs Hussey was stuffing shortbread biscuits into her at an awful rate. As soon as Mrs Peters was stopped talking, she started up with the suggestion she'd come to make to me. And she says it as if to ease the blow Mrs Peters had just dealt. "I..." she started and swallowed a large mouthful of biscuit, "I...or the Church Committee and I had an idea," she says. (Though she was speaking to me, she kept her eyes on Mrs Peters.) "Next Sunday is Whit Sunday and Father O'Kane is planning a Folk Mass for the day. Anybody who is anybody in the parish is taking part in it, bringing up the offerings or whatever. And we thought, as a way of saying goodbye to everybody, you might like to drop the flowers from the balcony."

"Drop the flowers?" I says to her, for I hadn't an inkling what she was talking about. And Mrs Peters pushed her plate back as if to say she had nothing to do with the idea. But Mrs Hussey was no way put about and explained to me what she was talking about. "In the old days," she says, "in some chapels, people dropped red roses from the balcony. The roses was to represent the tongues of flame. And Father O'Kane says we ought to do the same in our chapel this year. It's so as people will mind the Mass better. The flowers is to be dropped when the Veni Sancte Spiritus is being sung."

Now this was just like young Father O'Kane with his high-flying notions. All the same, I agreed to do what Mrs Hussey says for I never let the Church down in my life before.

"That's that then," she says, obviously relieved, and sprung up off her chair to go. But Mrs Peters wasn't finished yet. No.

181

She wanted a tour about the place. And Mrs Hussey—aye afraid to miss a bar—invited herself along as well, and made a nuisance of herself sticking her nose in wardrobes and other places she had no business being. The house was that empty our voices sounded through the rooms and come back at us in eerie echoes. Every room we went in, I couldn't help but think of the life Father and me had lived there. The memory wasn't gone, just buried in the walls with all the other lives was lived there before we come. It only took the right person to see that. And I think Mrs Peters seen it for she was respectful and quiet, the way you would be in a chapel.

I thought to myself the disciples must've felt the same way I was feeling, gathered the-gether in that room after Jesus was gone. They must've been wondering what to do next, the same way I was wondering what to do without Father. And they must've been feared for their lives, too, the way I was feared for my life. I thought back over the house as Father and me had had it. I minded the big black head of the Saint Martin that stared out the front window like a terrible guard on patrol. It was that black, it scared the wits out of Tim's wee grand-daughter. And the statue of the Virgin that aye stood at the foot of Father's bed. She wasn't a hate the worse for the knocking about Father had given her in the end. Though some splinters was missing, I'd managed to stick the head back in its place. Nobody could ever tell the difference so long as she was set with her back to the wall. I minded the way she used to watch over me every morning when I was making the bed; as if to make sure I was tucking the sheets in right and putting Father's pyjamas in the proper place. When we walked in the room that day, I felt she was still there, looking over us, like Our Lady of Lourdes. Father's study was dreary. All that was left there was a stack of old *Ireland's Own* that Damon hadn't thought it worth his while to take away.

I knew every spot in the carpet in that house (and there was plenty of them) and everything that was spilled on them. I knew every patch in the wallpaper the way you'd know your own skin. I knew every window needed a new hasp and every door that needed a new lock. You get to know a house like that and learn to live with it. But outsiders coming in just see the things in need of change.

Apart from the kitchen and the living room, my own was the only other room left in use. This may seem rare to you, but it never crossed my mind to move into Father's old room even though his room was the biggest and best in the place and caught the sunlight for most of the day. It wouldn't have felt right, you know what I mean. And, anyway, I had to think what the Bishop would say.

My room was in a shameful state. There was clothes everywhere. And I hadn't even made the bed. What was the point, I says to myself, when there wasn't nobody to see; or nobody but me? And, in the mood I was in, I couldn't've cared less what kind of a mess it was in. The mattress was bare. It was clay-brown in colour, I mind, with big yellow sunflowers on it. Whenever she seen this, Mrs Peters says she'd seen enough.

"Next Sunday, then," she says and looked me straight in the eye. She was a woman of few words, this Mrs Peters, and says no more than got the business done. And, if you want my opinion, she didn't like the job she was doing neither; not like Mrs Hussey who enjoyed herself walking over people. God, but power is a terrible thing. I didn't hold it against Mrs Peters when she told me I had to go. She was just the messenger. And she says, as well, she'd look me up whenever I settled some place else. I knew she wouldn't, of course. Her and me was from different worlds. She'd been lucky. But I decided to give her Dympna's address just in case. The only thing I could find to write it on was a photo of Father that Tim had taken the year before. And I wrote it on the back of this. When I handed her the photo, I noticed a look of embarrassment flit across her face. I knew the reason, too. For Father looked like a puffed-up idiot in that picture. Indeed, he aye come over like Lord Muck when you put a camera in front of him; at least, since he got sick, he did. I mind the day that particular picture was taken. He pushed me out of the road (for Tim had meant me to be in the picture as well) and stuck his chest out like a peacock. With his lapels pulled back like that, he looked a proper mockery of the Sacred Heart.

The grounds and garden about the house was all overgrown since Father went away. The way things was, the Church would only pay for the upkeep of the place so long as a priest was staying there. And anyone else, like me, was expected to look after the place themselves. I didn't bother myself, of course. Though you're likely thinking I should've done—that it would've been healthy for me to keep my mind busy and my hands full. But let me tell you something. Leaving it to go wild was a kind of protest, like the civil riots, as far as I was concerned. And I'll tell you the reason why as well. I felt like a woman whose husband had died. And nobody was taking any heed of me. Not another living soul in the parish or out of it seen Father's leaving the way I did. To their way of thinking, I hadn't the right to mourn. So I let the place run to rack and ruin to get my own back and get the notice I wanted. It was a proper jungle by the time Mrs Peters set eyes on it. The roses Tim had planted in February was strangled. At the time, I figured Tim must've stopped looking after them because the

Bishop wasn't paying him any longer. But he says after he was scared stiff to come near the place since I wouldn't let him in the door. (Tim was aye like that; weak-spirited when it come to the crunch. The tiniest hint of trouble and he was off like a march-hare. He was never one for the chase neither. That was another thing bothered me about him. People wasn't worth it in his view.) I'm sure Mrs Peters noticed the state of the place though she didn't say nothing to me about it. Instead, she picked her step as best she could, and Mrs Hussey after her. I left the pair of them to the gate. Mrs Hussey wished me all the best. And, except Mrs Peters was there, I swear I would've rammed the words back down her throat. Words cost nothing.

The waiting had been the worst. I seen that now. The word I had to leave didn't shake me the way I thought it would've done. Now it had happened, the anger and fear just drained away and a rare stillness come over me. Not but I've undergone the same transformation since and can tell you better now what done it to me. It was like this; once I got over the brink of what scared the devil out of me, the dread and fear just went away on account I'd seen the worst of it. My whole life with Father was spent standing on the brink shivering for fear I'd lose him by some stroke of fate and have to fare on my own. I'd never fared on my own, you see, and I didn't think I could manage it. I'd aye taken myself for a coward 'cos other people says I was a coward, from the girls at school to Tim in recent times. But this day, when I seen I was finally on my own, I didn't feel scared any more. I felt a courage I didn't know I had before come from somewhere deep inside myself. The courage to make whatever decisions had to be made, to do whatever had to be done to save myself. To hell with the Catholic Church! I says. In this mood, I didn't want to go back inside the house. Anyway, it looked like a prison from where I was standing with the curtains pulled over, like sleeping eyes, and the moss which was covering the roof and walls. I was desperate to do something, though. Then it was I noticed an old bill hook under a crab-apple tree in the corner of the garden. Tim must've thrown it behind him the last time he was working here. And I started cutting the jungle back with this. I wasn't doing it for Mrs Peters neither, nor for Father's sake, God bless him. I was doing it for me. For the first time in my life, I was doing something for me. Time just disappeared. About five hours later, Tim was passing on his way from the fields, and he slowed down when he seen me hard at it with the hook. Poor man, he was in swithers whether to come in or not. I suppose you couldn't blame him after the cold shoulder I'd given him. In the end he worked up the nerve, though he just hung round a while without saying a word to me. I didn't say a word to him neither. We just looked at one another a minute or so. Then I hacked away a rhododendron bush was getting out of hand and cleared the grass round the rose-bed in the corner. It was him that spoke up first.

To tempt me, he says, "That's hardly a woman's job."

"Who says so?" says I.

"At least let me give you a hand," he says.

We worked another hour till I was so parched I was ready to drop off my feet.

There was nothing in the house to drink but some altar wine that Father had left behind him. I set the hook down on the kitchen table.

"Where's the glasses?" Tim says to me

There wasn't any. Damon had taken the lot of them. So we drank out of china cups instead, having dispensed with the saucers first. Sitting there that day, with the hook at my left hand and the cup of altar wine in my right, I felt for the first time I wasn't a priest's maid any more. And it made me happy— real happy. I was well able to look after myself now. You only had to look at the garden to see that. And I didn't care the wine I was knocking back was altar wine. Tim held off, though. When I asked him why, he says he didn't like me carrying on.

"Carrying on?" says I.

"Aye! Smart-acting," says he.

God! There was no pleasing him. In the first place, he didn't like it when I was Father's doormat. And now I was acting like my own person, he didn't like that any more. Some people is never satisfied.

The wine tasted sour. But, after two cups, I hardly noticed or cared neither; for I was pleased with the effect it was having on me. Drink's a good thing. As Father Jack used to say, it loosens the tongue. I told Tim what Mrs Hussey had suggested for the Folk Mass.

"They'll have a dove flying over the faithful too, I suppose," he says. (That was another thing they done besides throwing flowers over the balcony.) I seen fine well Tim was in a mocking mood. "You don't mean to tell me you're going to do it?" he growls at me.

I told him I wasn't certain. Sure enough, I'd no time left for the Bishop any more, and I'd resigned myself to living without Father. But I didn't know if I could give up God that easy. And I says as much to Tim.

"You got to be your own God, Brigid." That was his advice to me. If the nuns or the Bishop heard him! "Take charge of your own life," he says. "Don't rely on some power outside yourself. All you got to do is get used to living without religion. Everybody's doing it nowadays."

This had to be the devil talking, I says to myself. Tim brought everything back to religion and he never give up trying to get me on his side. I don't think he ever forgive me for choosing Father over him. I mind, as well, the angry way he looked that day. His lips was wet with the altar wine and his eyes was blazing. Once he started on religion, there was no stopping him.

Says he, "People is overcome by religion. It tells them who to be and what to do. It makes life simple."

"Well, isn't that a good thing?" says I, for I was aye one for keeping things simple.

"No!" says he, real sharp. I could see he was losing his temper with me. "Life isn't that simple. People's way of thinking is changing that fast nowadays. Catholic religion, as you and me know it, is out of date. Take the matter of divorce."

So this is where he was leading. He wanted to dump Matty and do it with an easy conscience. But I wasn't going to give him Absolution; and, more, I wasn't going to be led astray by him. The little faith I had was my only comfort. And be damned, if I was going to let go of it for him.

"Give it up, Brigid," he says.

"I can't," says I. How could I when the Catholic Church had looked after me for over fifty years. More than most Catholics, my day, my week, my year had been shaped by Father and religion. Now, the way Tim was talking, every day would be the same and there'd be nothing to look forward to at the end of it. I couldn't bear the thought of that. As I seen it, life didn't make sense without God.

"Who says it's got to make sense?" he says.

"Don't talk nonsense," says I. "Everything has to make sense."

"Nonsense," says he.

"Who are you trying to talk round," says I, "yourself or me?" For he was arguing that hard. And when his shouting didn't get him nowhere, he lowered his voice and tried the wily approach. "It's a grand-scam," says he. "You know you don't believe it. You never believed it."

"I did. I did." I roared back at him that hard it hurt my tonsils. This kind of shouting wasn't like me at all and I put it down to the altar wine.

He grinned. "You think you believed," says he, "and you know you don't believe any more." His eyes was staring straight through me whenever he says this.

Who was I trying to fool? It didn't need Tim to turn me about for I could do that right well on my own. I could hear this small voice whispering inside my own head. "I don't believe. I never believed." It grew louder and louder. Still I clung on, desperate, like a body was drowning. If there was a thunderstorm before eight o'clock that night, I says to myself, I'd believe in God forever after. I'd take it as a sign from Heaven.

"I'm waiting for a sign," I says to Tim.

Well, that drove him demented. "Jesus," he roars out of him. "What more signs do you want, woman? Look at y'rsell! Look what your precious religion has done to you. What kind of a sign is that, eh, Brigid? Could you tell me what that sign means?"

I was still waiting for the thunderstorm.

Says he, "I'll tell you what that sign means. Your Catholic Church, with its man-God, expects a woman to keep her mouth shut. To keep her mouth shut and serve. And that's what you've been doing all these years—all these years you could've been living a full life for y'rsell."

This was jealousy talking and I says as much to him.

"Jealous of your Father Mann?" he says with a big laugh. "You must think I'm an idiot, Brigid. I pitied him. I pity any man as had to go through what he went through. But I don't blame them. I blame the Church that nabbed them as youngsters—poor brats, dragged from their homes before they had sense enough to know better, before they had time to grow up. They're brainwashed in Maynooth, you know. Read the Bible over dinner, day in, day out, till they can't think or speak nothing else. They're not allowed to talk and yell at one another like normal youngsters. Poor bastards. In the end they get so they can't open their mouth to a living soul. Not properly speaking, anyway. They don't know how. And they're put into little black uniforms, this little Army of the Lord. Your beloved Father Mann was one of them. Jealous of him? You must be joking."

Tim had always hated the clergy. I knew that much already. But what he says this day affected me in spite of myself. I couldn't get out of my head the way the Bishop had dumped me. Up till then, I'd aye expected him to look after me. And when I lost faith in him, I lost faith in everything else he stood for and that included God. I stared into the mucky sediment of the altar wine in the bottom of the cup.

"Want another?" Tim says and holds out the bottle to me.

I rinsed away the slurry and held the cup out to him. "Fill it to the top," says I. The wine carried me along with it, slowly and surely over the edge of sobriety. It was like falling off a cliff backward in slow motion knowing for sure there's enough water below to cushion your fall. At the same time my insides tightened for fear of losing a grip on myself. My head was bursting. But it wasn't the wine alone was responsible. The rage

190

which deserted me earlier had come back again with a vengeance. The wine and talk had managed to resurrect it. That night, drink proved stronger than religion. It filled me—not with love, as altar wine is supposed to do—but with hate. Hate for the Bishop, for Father, and hate for the people in the parish that had turned their back on me; hate for all the people that had used me and abused me down the years, and all in the name of religion. I didn't give a damn if God heard what I was saying. All the things I was dying to say to the Bishop's face for years, but hadn't the guts to say, come spilling out of me. I cursed him as a woman-hater, a two-faced liar and a prig. God love poor Tim; he had to listen to it all. Nor did it stop at talk. I grabbed a hold of the hook and brought it crashing down on the table in front of me. Tim jumped out of his seat! But not before a splinter caught him in the eye. If he hadn't grabbed a hold of me, I swear, I would've hacked the table to bits. My temper was that bad.

The fit was over soon enough. God, but anger takes it out of you. And I dropped down in my chair again and fired the hook to the other end of the room. The muscles in Tim's face relaxed.

"You've had enough," says he when I filled the cup another time. But I didn't pay him any heed. I hadn't rid myself of one man telling me what to do to land myself with another. My mind was running on all sorts of things, mainly to do with Father and me and why I ever come to work for him in the first place.

"I've been guilty of pride," says I to Tim.

He winced. "I don't want to hear your Confession, Brigid," he says.

"Father McFaul," I laughed at him.

He poured what wine was left in his own cup back into the bottle.

"It suits you," says I. "Go on. Hear me out. I'm giving you a chance to be what you always wanted to be. A priest," says I, "only you didn't have religion."

He shook his finger at me like he was scowling a wayward youngster. "Don't mock about things like that, Brigid," he says.

I took the bottle back. "Just hear me out," I says.

"I don't like you when you're like this," says he.

"Like what?" says I, as sharp as you like, for I didn't like him coming over all high and mighty with me. Who was he to judge?

The drunker I got, the more sober Tim become. He didn't even talk the same. "I don't know who you are," says he. "You're not steady."

"Well," says I, "you know where to go if you want somebody steady. Go back home to Matty. She's steady as a rock. You may be sure where her mind's at—on the calves in need of gelding or the beasts in need of worming."

Tim didn't like me talking about Matty in that way. It was all well and fine so long as he was doing the scowling. But another person...

"One minute you say one thing," says he, "and another minute you say another. You're not making sense."

"Who says I got to make sense?" says I, getting back at him for what he says about religion earlier.

He got tired fighting all of a sudden. "Ahh," he growled, as if to throw me off and huddled his head between his shoulders. He looked terrible pathetic. And I offered to fill his cup again. But, the kind of Tim, he didn't have it in him to get drunk, or so I thought at the time. Getting drunk would've been a come down for the likes of him. Tim liked to be in charge, you see.

"I been guilty of pride," I says, starting all over again.

"So you keep telling me," he says.

But this time I didn't give a damn whether he paid me any heed or not. I was in a mood to talk and I was going to talk. I since seen a man in a bar talk happily to the air in front of him for two whole hours. Then what else was I doing all them years I thought I was praying to God? We all need somebody to talk to, least I do. "I stayed with Father," I says, "because he made me feel good about myself. You might say I had the pride of Mary. Mind her words. 'All generations shall call me blessed; because He who is powerful hath done great things for me.' The fact is," I says to Tim, "I used Father just the same way he used me."

Tim checked his watch and got up from his seat. "I got to go," he says. "Matty'll be waiting on me. You know what she's like." And he backed out of the room, like a scared mongrel making a getaway. Not that I cared whether he stayed or went by this stage. People only get in my way when I've a drop taken. They stop me talking to myself. That day, I was happy mulling over all the things had led me to my present predicament; things I let pass without a thought at the time they happened, but took on a new kind of meaning for me now. Like the time a young nun with a very beautiful face had leaned over my cot in Bethel House. Looking back, that tiny incident seemed to me like the visitation of Our Lady to Bernadette. Only the nun's beautiful face and her hands had showed under her heavy black habit. But her hands was lovely, the kind you could almost see through; not like my own was now. I looked down at my own hands. They were red and swollen with strong detergents, and twisted with the beginnings of arthritis. This was the price of thirty-three years in Father's service. I minded the same young nun standing in a ray of very bright sunlight. She must've gone from the convent after that for I never seen her again. Though I asked about her, years later, nobody would tell me anything about her. What she was doing in my head thirty-three years on, I couldn't say.

I minded, as well, the terrible babble of voices in the dorm of Bethel House. When I was a youngster, I mind, I couldn't make myself heard over this racket. That night, I could hear them voices again, babbling on and on in my head, though I couldn't make out a sensible word they says. The sounds was just noise and nonsense to me.

Minding things is all fine and well for a while, but I couldn't thole it for very long. So I buried myself in one of Father's old *Ireland's Owns*. And it was here I come on the picture of an old steamer leaving the port of Derry for Liverpool. Beneath the picture was an article about the people that left Derry at the time of the last world war. Most of them never come back. The year on the picture was nineteen-forty-two; the year I was born. Here was a sign, I says to myself, for I'd given up on the thunderstorm by this time and was on the look out for some other sign to show me the way. I had money enough to get me there and keep me a couple of weeks till I got a job. There was no doubt in my mind but I'd find work waiting for me on the other side. For wasn't there plenty of jobs in England? Isn't that what people was always saying?

You may know, I hadn't a leg to stand on the following morning after drinking that much altar wine. It was about dinner time when I dragged myself out of my bed, or fell out, to be more accurate. My head was splitting and my teeth was sticking the-gether. The insides of my mouth tasted rotten. But these things was nothing to the terrible guilt I was feeling. It was that bad, I may tell you, I wanted more drink to take it away. Thanks be to God there wasn't any left, otherwise I might've started all over again. And God alone knows where that would've landed me. I'd drunk the whole lot, even the slurry was in the bottom of the bottle. But, hold on, I says to myself, I couldn't mind finishing it. I couldn't mind going to bed neither. God, says I, I've got Alzheimer's disease. Scared as I was, it wasn't the fear of Alzheimer's got the better of me, but the guilt I was feeling. That was the thing I couldn't get out of my mind; that and the shame of Tim seeing me the way he did. I needed to go to Confession. Then I minded I didn't believe in God any more. Still, I needed to talk to somebody—anybody. I needed to see Father O'Kane anyway, to tell him I wouldn't be taking part in the Whitsun Mass. So I decided to have a word with him.

The three miles into Dungiven felt like thirty-three, my head was that light. Wee Father was busy when I got as far as the Presbytery. I had it "in confidence" from his maid he was trying to talk a woman out of leaving her husband and weans. (Poor woman! I knew the man and I didn't blame her.)

"But you won't breathe a word, not to a living soul," says Mrs Chambers in a low voice, in my ear. That woman should've been fired. She had no business being a priest's maid, telling yarns behind people's backs like that. You'd never've caught me telling stories; not in all the years I worked for Father.

I told her I'd wait for I had nothing else to do anyway. It was rare, sitting there watching another woman running round the house after a priest the way I used to do. And it set me thinking again about all the years and all the life I'd given Father.

"Been up to the chapel, recently?" Mrs Chambers says as she handed me a cup of tea. (Just tea; no bread or biscuits.) She likely knew I hadn't been, and only asked me out of badness.

"No," says I and left it at that. For, as I'd come round to discovering, I didn't owe her nor nobody no explanations for what I done. I was my own master, as they say.

"The flowers they put on the altar for Whitsun is the finest I ever seen," she says. "I seen the bill for them. Forty-five pound, would you believe. But you won't be breathing a word to nobody."

Forty-five pounds, I thought to myself. Nobody never spent a penny on flowers for me. And the more I thought on it, the angrier I got.

Father O'Kane didn't keep me waiting long. Then he had a name for being speedy. The saying was, round Dungiven, he had ten minutes for a marriage in trouble, five minutes for a drunkard and no time for anybody contradicted him. I was just about to tell him the reason I'd come when he took the foreroad of me.

"You'll be needing money for the roses," he says, and he produced a money box. He kept the key hid behind a Bible on the mantlepiece, I noticed. The way he opened the money box, honest to God, you'd think something inside was going to take the hand off him. He tried to hide the money, but I seen right well the big wad of notes he had. And it was then I decided I'd do what the Church Committee wanted after all.

"How much will you need?" he says.

"Thirty," says I, "like the thirty pieces of silver."

He looked at me like I was rare. "I'll need a receipt for this," he says; and he counted out the thirty pounds a second time before he give it to me. "It's not that I don't trust you, you understand. But the Church Committee... "

The nerve of him! Like I was going to run off and buy a new frock with it, or a bottle of gin. Not that I wasn't entitled, mind you. I wouldn't even try to put a figure on the amount the Church owed me.

I rung Tim next. It was Matty answered and she gave me the blunt edge of her tongue. God, but that woman was awful thick. When Tim come on the other end, I knew from the sound of his voice she'd given him a touch. Still, there was no call letting it out on me. "What do you want?" he gowls at me.

"Could you give me a lift?" says I.

"I'm busy, Brigid," he snaps back.

"Not now. Sunday," says I. "Can you wait for me outside the chapel gate."

"But you're going Sunday," he says to me.

"Aye," I told him. "I'm leaving after Sunday Mass."

"You up to something?" he says. For I'm sure he could hear the excitement in my voice. But I says nothing.

"I don't want to get into trouble with anyone, the clergy 'specially," he warned me.

"Don't worry," says I.

"Ten then," says he and put the phone down.

Between then and Sunday I was happy just imagining Father O'Kane's face; and the Bishop's, most of all, when the story got to him.

Whitsun was a hot May day that year, I mind. I'd got a special dress for the occasion. Deep red silk, it was, with black undertones and satin trimmings. I got some looks that day, I can tell you. People had put me down as a dowdy old maid before; not that I could blame them, for I'd stopped taking care of myself after I thought men wasn't interested in me any more.

Mrs Chambers was right, the altar did look grand, all decked out with tulips and chrysanthemums. I was early at the chapel, well before anyone else, and I brought the flowers with me. The

197

first thing I did was check out where I was supposed to be on the balcony. There was two ways up, one beside the altar and one beside the back door. I went up. And I was sitting up here, just thinking to myself, when a dark, good-looking young fella come in underneath. I knew him right away for Father Jack's nephew. He must've been one of the band for he was carrying a guitar under his arm. Thinking he had the place to himself, he plugged in his guitar and started to play. Even I knew that was no hymn he was playing. The next thing he took out a cigarette and started to smoke. Between puffs, he'd stick the cigarette in the head of the guitar. A thin trickle of smoke, like incense, rose from the burning cigarette into the air. He let rip with all his might and filled the chapel full of music. I let him play a good ten minutes before I let him know I was there. Indeed, I managed to get up close to him before he noticed; for he had his eyes closed and his mind was lost in the music.

"Jesus!" he started as soon as he seen me. (Maybe he smelt my perfume. Le Jardin, it was. I'd bought it with the dress.) He mumbled, "I'm sorry," a couple of times and his face went beetroot red with shame.

"It's all right," I says. "I won't breathe a word to a living soul."

He looked at me a moment. "Do I know you from somewhere?" he says.

"I used to be maid to Father Mann," I says.

"Sorry," says he again. (He made a terrible habit of saying sorry.) "I didn't know you. You're that done up."

The cigarette he'd been smoking was all but burned out by this time. And, cool as you like, he stubbed the butt out against his fingertips. I couldn't believe my eyes. He laughed. "They're hardened," says he. "See." And he held out the fingers to me.

Sure enough, the skin was tough as leather. "Here," says he, "try for yourself." And he handed me the cigarette.

"They have to be hard," he says, "otherwise I couldn't play." And he let rip again. But, this time he kept his eyes on me. "My uncle Jack used to talk about you," he says.

I asked him what his uncle Jack had to say.

"Ah, that would be telling," says he with a grin. "But you know Jack. Always an eye for the women."

Unless I was mistaken, this young fella was flirting with me; and me old enough to be his mother. Then you get some young fellas like that—prefer older women to girls their own age. Father Mann was one; though, the kind of him, he'd never let on. I mind the kind caught his eye when he thought nobody was looking. But that was a long time back, when I went to work for him at the start. This young fella minded me a bit on Father the way he was the very first time ever I set eyes on him.

At ten on the dot, Father O'Kane appeared on the altar. The band struck up and the whole congregation started singing "Morning has broken like the first morning." It was just too much sound to fill that tiny chapel. Wee Father O'Kane launched into the opening prayer. "I will not leave you orphans..." With the sound of his voice drumming in my ears, I undid the wrapper from the roses and stepped close to the balcony. The Collect and the Epistle was both read by the headmaster of Saint Mary's. Then Mrs Hussey stepped primly up to the rostrum to say the Alleluia. The sound of the Choir starting up the Veni Sancte Spiritus was my cue to drop the roses. And I flung them for all my worth over the congregation. In the excitement of the moment some of the choir lost their places. Their voices become a confused babble. And I could hear Father O'Kane's broken voice getting louder and louder as he tried to guide them back on the right track again. I slipped down the back stairs in the meantime. At the back door, I caught young Fraggart's eye. And he winked back at me. Tim was waiting outside like I had asked him to. His car, an old beat up Rover, had a big dinge in the front of it. "Jump in," he says.

I smelt the drink off his breath right away. Unlike Father Jack, he couldn't put it down to altar-wine that time on a Sunday morning. "Where to?" he says.

"Father O'Kane's first," I told him.

"But there'll be nobody in," says he, as if I didn't know as much myself and me after leaving the wee Father and Mrs Chambers in the chapel.

Patsy—that's Father Jack's maid—had told me one time where Mrs Chambers left the key. And I found it where she says; under a stone at the front door. In my heart of hearts I was hoping the money wouldn't be there. But it was, and a lot more with it. The whole lot filled my handbag.

"Where now?" says Tim when I come out again.

"I'm catching the boat-train for England," I says to him.

He got mad as hell. And I knew the reason why as well. The kind of Tim, it made him angry to see another person doing what he hadn't the guts to do himself.

He plagued me with question after question. The Inquisition wouldn't be in it with him. Till, in the end, he got on my nerves, for I wasn't able to put my thoughts in words the way he wanted me to. Not that I owed him any explanation. All I knew was I wanted out of there. The place was smothering me. And I says as much to him. He shut up then.

We come into Derry by Bridge-End and along the Culmore Road. The streets was deserted as was usual on a Sunday. For years now, since the Troubles started, the place was a ghost town after the shops shut on Saturday night. An army jeep crawled by and the soldier on Tim's side gave him a suspicious look. There was a light on in the Odeon in the Strand but everyplace else was shuttered and dark. In the Guildhall Square the only sign of life was some rubbish blowing in the wind which only made the place look more desolate and deserted. Barely visible behind a barrage of shutters, the Foyle Street bus-station was shut up for the day. The way things was, nobody in Derry had any business outside their own front door on a Sunday except to go to church or chapel. I took heed of a lone woman loitering at the foot of Orchard Street, like she was waiting on somebody. She stared in at us as we passed.

"Ahh," Tim let a growl out of him. "You're likely better out of this God-forsaken place. Do you mind it, in the Fifties," he says, "when you and me was growing up? You wouldn't think to look at it now. Mind—Shipquay Street teeming with life at night. Brightly lit shops and people out having a good time. Six cinemas there was, can you believe it? Not to mention the Corinthian Ballroom in Bishop Street, and the Embassy in the Strand. And Yannarelli's fish and chip shop. That was in the Strand too, do you mind? People wasn't afraid to leave their houses then."

Tim was in a right miserable mood that day. But there was something to his story still and all. Derry was far from the place it used to be when him and me was growing up. Like me, it was worn down by strife and trouble; though I never ceased to marvel at the way it kept rearing its head no matter how many times it was flattened. At the same time, I wasn't sorry to be leaving the place. Just surviving wasn't enough for me any more.

At the checkpoint on the bridge, a policeman with a pistol

signalled us to stop. He took Tim's licence across to a soldier was standing on the other side of the road. They talked for a few minutes. Then the soldier come across and started firing questions at us. Was Tim and me married? What work did Tim do? Where was I going? Like it was any of his business! I worried if he decided to hold us up and search the car I'd miss my train.

The last impression I have of Derry was Tim cadging a light off a conductor on the platform. Then he drew his cheeks in till they were hollow. And I turned my face away.